Gray needed to get Kathryn on his side.

He half smiled, plans for soliciting Miss Seeger's help spinning through his head. He would pay the lovely lady a visit, apologize profusely for barging into her store and then beg her to help him. He'd been told he wasn't without charm. If he remembered how to use that charm, he might be able to convince the boutique owner, *the really pretty boutique owner,* that Ashley's wedding was a bad idea and it was her duty to bow out of the plans.

Gray frowned, realizing it was the third or fourth time since leaving the boutique that he had thought about Kathryn Seeger in terms of her attractiveness. Her appeal didn't matter. It couldn't. All that mattered right now was putting an end to his baby sister's wedding.

Well, that was the original plan, anyway....

Dear Reader,

March is a month of surprises and a time when we wait breathlessly for the first hints of spring. A young man's fancy is beginning to turn to love...but then, in each Special Edition novel, thoughts of love are everywhere! And March has a whole bouquet of love stories for you!

I'm so pleased to announce that *Waiting for Nick* by Nora Roberts is coming your way this month. This heartwarming story features Freddie finally getting her man...the man she's been waiting for all of her life. Revisit the Stanislaskis in this wonderful addition to Nora Roberts's bestselling series, THOSE WILD UKRAINIANS.

If handsome rogues quicken your pulse, then don't miss *Ashley's Rebel* by Sherryl Woods. This irresistible new tale is the second installment of her new series, THE BRIDAL PATH. And Diana Whitney concludes her PARENTHOOD series this month—with *A Hero's Child*, an emotionally stirring story of lovers reunited in a most surprising way.

Three veteran authors return this month with wonderful new romances. Celeste Hamilton's *Marry Me in Amarillo* will warm your heart, and Carole Halston dazzles her readers once again with *The Wrong Man...The Right Time*. Kaitlyn Gorton' newest, *Separated Sisters,* showcases this talented writer's gift of portraying deep emotion with the joy of lasting love.

I hope that you enjoy this book, and each and every story to come!

Sincerely,

Tara Gavin,

Senior Editor

Please address questions and book requests to:
Silhouette Reader Service
U.S.: 3010 Walden Ave., P.O. Box 1325, Buffalo, NY 14269
Canadian: P.O. Box 609, Fort Erie, Ont. L2A 5X3

CELESTE HAMILTON

MARRY ME IN AMARILLO

SPECIAL EDITION®

Published by Silhouette Books
America's Publisher of Contemporary Romance

For Maureen Moran,
in appreciation of her encouragement
and continued support

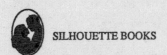

SILHOUETTE BOOKS

ISBN 0-373-24091-0

MARRY ME IN AMARILLO

This edition published by arrangement with Harlequin Books S.A.

® and TM are trademarks of Harlequin Books S.A., used under license. Trademarks indicated with ® are registered in the United States Patent and Trademark Office, the Canadian Trade Marks Office and in other countries.

Printed in U.S.A.

Books by Celeste Hamilton

Silhouette Special Edition

Torn Asunder #418
Silent Partner #447
A Fine Spring Rain #503
Face Value #532
No Place To Hide #620
Don't Look Back #690
Baby, It's You #708
Single Father #738
Father Figure #779
Child of Dreams #827
Sally Jane Got Married #865
Which Way Is Home? #897
A Family Home #938
The Daddy Quest #994
Marry Me in Amarillo #1091

Silhouette Desire

*The Diamond's Sparkle #537
*Ruby Fire #549
*The Hidden Pearl #561

*Aunt Eugenia's Treasures trilogy

Montana Mavericks

Man Without a Past

CELESTE HAMILTON

has been writing since she was ten years old, with the encouragement of parents who told her she could do anything she set out to do and teachers who helped her refine her talents.

The broadcast media captured her interest in high school, and she graduated from the University of Tennessee with a B.S. in Communications. From there, she began writing and producing commercials at a Chattanooga, Tennessee, radio station.

Celeste began writing romances in 1985 and now works at her craft full-time. Married to a policeman, she likes nothing better than spending time at home with him and their two much-loved cats, although she and her husband also enjoy traveling when their busy schedules permit. Wherever they go, however, "It's always nice to come home to East Tennessee—one of the most beautiful corners of the world."

Blue Heaven Weddings

Amarillo, Texas,
USA

Specializing in:

Exquisite Bridal Gowns

Succulent West Texas Feasts

Exemplary Celebrations of All Kinds

Fairy-Tale Endings

"Dream Weddings Are Our Specialty"

Chapter One

What a beautiful bride.

Kathryn Seeger repeated the clichéd phrase to herself as she contemplated the gorgeous young woman standing before the dressing-room mirror. Kathryn, who dressed brides and planned weddings for a living, knew she should be immune to the sentiment of moments like this. But she wasn't. When she saw a gown this perfect, worn by a woman with love and excitement shining in her face, she was always moved to tears.

"Oh, my," she murmured as she blinked away the moisture in her eyes. "This dress was made for you."

Young Ashley Grant turned from the mirror, her pretty features glowing beneath the lace-and-net veil Kathryn had placed on her long, curling blond hair. "It's the wedding dress I've always dreamed of. How did you know?"

Kathryn smiled and gestured for Ashley to follow

her. "Come out in the showroom. I want you to see the back of the dress in the big mirror."

Moments later, Ashley stood on a dais in front of the huge gilt-framed, triple mirror that dominated the front showroom of Blue Heaven Weddings. Here, Ashley could fully appreciate the way the dress fell in pure white swirls of chiffon and lace from the tight, fitted waist. In the bright May sunshine that spilled through the broad windows, tiny beads and sequins shimmered and winked from the embroidered flowers on the skirt, from the snug bodice and the big, flat bow that accented the back just below the waist. Kathryn found long, lace gloves to complement the off-the-shoulder neckline and cap sleeves. Then she handed Ashley one of the silk bouquets the boutique kept on hand and stood back to admire the full impact of the ensemble.

Oohs and aahs came from the shop's other customers, a mother and daughter being waited on by Kathryn's associate, Devon Long.

"Your mother will cry when she sees you in this," Devon told Ashley.

The young bride-to-be smiled, yet Kathryn saw a flicker of sadness move over her features. In the hour and a half since Ashley had arrived at the boutique, Kathryn had learned the young woman's mother had passed away several years ago; her father wasn't part of her life, and on her eighteenth birthday, just a few months back, Ashley had received an inheritance from her mother's estate. The only stipulation attached to the money was that Ashley should use it for something she desired with all her heart.

"And I want a dream wedding," Ashley had told Kathryn. "Everyone says you do the best weddings in West Texas, so that's why I'm here." Flashing the diamond ring given to her by the son of a ranching family Kathryn knew quite well, Ashley looked young and beautiful and full of dreamy plans for cakes and bridesmaid gowns, trousseaus and honeymoons.

Personal experience had tempted Kathryn to advise Ashley to spend her considerable inheritance for rent and school. But it wasn't Kathryn's job to douse the fires of romantic enthusiasm with the cold water of reality. So she had shown Ashley photos of cakes, swatches of material, examples of invitations and many styles of gowns. For one so young, Ashley was remarkably mature, decisive and surprisingly frugal. She might be planning the wedding of her dreams for late August, but she wasn't being extravagant. Except with this dress. And when she had put on this gown, Kathryn had felt that moment of triumph she felt with most of her customers, that sense that she, in some small part, had helped them fulfill their fantasies.

Dream weddings were Kathryn's specialty.

For everyone but herself.

She shook out a fold in Ashley's skirt while she shrugged off that last, intrusive thought. She might sell nuptial fantasies to others, but she didn't buy them herself. She wasn't about to put herself under the control of matrimony or the power of a man. Not ever again.

The bell on the front door jangled with sudden impatience. A tall, muddy-booted man came across the room with a wide-eyed little boy trailing behind him. The two of them looked as out of place amid the frills and ruffles and ornate Victorian accents of Kathryn's shop as a couple of steers at a debutante ball. Eyes wide, the mother and daughter customers retreated with Devon to the desk where they had been discussing reception hors d'oeuvres. Kathryn just stared at the males in speechless shock as they strode toward Ashley.

"What in the hell is this?" the man growled, gesturing at the young beauty.

"My wedding dress." Chin lifted, Ashley gave the skirt an impertinent swish. "Isn't it beautiful?"

The man's features hardened. "When are you going to cut out this foolishness?"

Before Ashley could reply, Kathryn gathered her wits about her. "Now, wait a minute, sir. What do you think—"

"This is my brother," Ashley cut in, her tone cold. "My *half* brother, Gray. He thinks he rules the world. Especially my world."

Gray's eyes thinned to ice blue slits. His gaze still on Ashley, he said to Kathryn, "I don't want to disrupt your business, miss. But Ashley is wasting your time. She isn't getting married."

Confused, Kathryn glanced at the diamond glittering on Ashley's left hand.

The younger woman thrust the ring toward her older brother. "I'm marrying Jarrett McMullen on Saturday, August 30. And there's not one thing you can do to stop me."

"You're still just a kid and so's McMullen."

"I'm eighteen, and he's twenty. We're of legal age to do whatever we want."

"But neither of you has any business getting married."

Ashley tossed her head. "Just because you're content to be alone—"

"Don't start that damn nonsense again," her brother interrupted, his voice rising. "This isn't about me. It's about you and that irresponsible fool who gave you that ring.''

"Don't you call Jarrett a fool," Ashley shouted.

Before Gray could make another heated reply, Kathryn stepped between them. "This isn't the place to be having this argument.'' The bell over the door jangled again, admitting another customer, even as the mother and daughter scampered out. Kathryn glared at Gray and Ashley and lowered her voice. "This is a boutique, not a family counseling center."

For the first time, Gray's gaze met hers. The contrast between his smoldering, light blue eyes and deeply tanned face was quite startling. Under his intense regard, Kathryn decided she now knew how bugs must feel when caught in a predator's web.

"I'm sorry about the scene," he said, obviously struggling with his anger. "But Ashley isn't getting married.''

"Yes, I am."

Noting the looks being sent their way by the new customer, Kathryn again jumped into the fray before the argument could intensify. "Perhaps you two should talk in my office." She pointed toward a door to the right.

"There's nothing to talk about," Gray said tightly.

But Ashley was already gathering up silken skirts and swirling toward the office.

Ashley's brother gave Kathryn another hard look, then said, "Sorry about this," before striding after her. The door closed behind him with a firm click.

Then the shouting match resumed in earnest.

Kathryn sent Devon to assist the new customer in browsing through mother-of-the-bride dresses, then started for her office to put an end to the muffled but still audible argument. Only a small figure seated in one of the shop's deeply cushioned blue-and-gold chairs made her pause.

With a world-weary shrug, the little boy who had followed Gray into the boutique looked up at Kathryn. "It's best to just let 'em fight it out."

The child, who looked to be seven or eight years old, had Gray's blue eyes and Ashley's blond hair. He had a smear of something that looked like chocolate on his cheek and one of the sweetest smiles Kathryn had ever seen.

She couldn't resist smiling back. "So I should just leave them alone?"

He nodded. "Ashley and Gray are always fighting. They get over it."

He called the man Gray, not Dad. "Who are you?" she asked, curious since she had assumed the boy was Gray's son.

"Rick Grant," the child replied, smiling again. "I'm Ashley's brother. Gray's, too. He's our half brother, but we never used to say that."

"Why not?" Kathryn asked, curiosity overcoming her normally discreet nature.

Rick shrugged again. "When we moved here last year, and Ashley started being mad at Gray, she started telling everyone he was our half brother and our guard."

Kathryn frowned. "He's a guard?"

"He's in charge of us."

"Your guardian?" Kathryn suggested.

"Yeah," Rick said. "Gray has always taken care of us. Only now Ashley wants to marry Jarrett and leave." The beatific smile momentarily disappeared,

leaving Kathryn with the feeling he was none too
pleased about his sister's impending marriage.

The angry voices in the room behind them grew
louder. Rick shot an uneasy glance toward the door.
Kathryn decided this insanity had continued long
enough. Since the new customer had quickly followed
the others out the door, Kathryn called Devon over,
told her to take Rick out back to the kitchen for a cold
drink, then entered the office.

She found Ashley and her brother in a classic face-
off. The young woman was yelling while Gray shook
his head, pausing only to interject an occasional
shouted, "No way, never, not on your life."

After several polite attempts to be heard, Kathryn
finally screamed, "Just shut up!"

Both Gray's and Ashley's heads snapped toward her.
Kathryn sucked in a deep, calming breath. "You're
going to have to take this discussion somewhere else."

"I'm sorry," Ashley muttered, hitching up her skirts
and heading for the door. "There's no discussing this
with him anyway."

A muscle twitched under her brother's right eye, but
he held his tongue. He and Ashley traded one last, baleful glare before she flounced out of the room.

The ensuing silence stretched for several moments
before Kathryn nervously cleared her throat. "Mr.
Grant..." she began.

"The name's Nolan. Gray Nolan," he said, his tone
clipped. "Ashley and I had the same mother. Different
fathers, different names."

"Mr. Nolan," Kathryn started again.

But he stalked past her before she could say anything
more. Kathryn frowned, thinking him as rude and dis-
agreeable as any man she had ever met. She was be-

ginning to sympathize with Ashley's plight. Squaring her jaw, Kathryn hurried out of the office. She didn't expect Gray Nolan to be standing just outside the door, else she wouldn't have plowed into his back.

He wheeled around, broad hands stretching out to steady her as she swayed from the impact of their collision.

"Excuse me," she mumbled, hurriedly stepping out of his warm grasp.

His clear blue eyes blazed down at her. "There isn't going to be a wedding."

Kathryn pulled back. "Mr. Nolan, I don't see—"

"No wedding," he repeated, his voice deep and authoritative. "Are you the owner here?"

"Well, yes, but—"

"I'm ordering you not to help her plan this nonsense."

"Ordering me?" Pain lanced Kathryn's temples. Until now she had been merely aggravated. There had been family squabbles in this boutique before. When dealing with highly emotional brides, grooms and their families, a person learned to take the occasional blowup in stride. But this man got under Kathryn's skin, as did most autocratic, overbearing men.

Gray Nolan's face was a determined mask. "She's not marrying that McMullen boy."

"*That* boy comes from one of Amarillo's finest families. They're good friends of mine."

"Fine or not, he's too young to be marrying her, and she's too young to be marrying anyone."

In all honesty, Kathryn agreed. But she just planned the weddings, she didn't encourage or discourage them. "I don't provide prenuptial counseling, Mr. Nolan."

"Oh, I know that." Reaching one long arm around

her, he pulled a lacy parasol out of an antique umbrella stand. "All you do is sell silly little bits of nonsense like this that young girls like Ashley think marriage is about. They don't see that once you get past the lace and the silk and the candlelight, there's a lot more to it."

"You're right." Kathryn rescued the fragile parasol from him, and resisted the urge to hit him over the head with it. "There's a lot more to it. But that's something I think you and Ashley should take up at home."

"Just so we understand each other," the big, angry man said. "You won't encourage her."

"Encourage her?" Kathryn repeated, the ache in her temples slowly becoming a roar. "Mr. Nolan, I never met Ashley before today."

"But you know McMullen's family."

"Yes, but even though I knew Jarrett McMullen was seeing someone pretty steadily, I never knew who it was until today. I didn't tell him to send his fiancée over here. Ashley came to me. And I can assure you that she needed no encouragement about wedding plans. She walked in that door knowing exactly what she wanted in a wedding. She's a very determined and self-assured young woman."

"Couldn't you see that she's too young to be engaged?"

"She's eighteen."

"She's a baby."

"And the more you say that, the more determined she's going to be to prove you wrong."

Gray Nolan did a double take. "What did you say?"

Kathryn hadn't intended to start giving advice. But in the face of this man's blind arrogance, she couldn't resist. "Ashley is not a baby. Not by a long shot. But if that's how you continue to treat her, she's going to do everything she can to thwart your efforts to keep her penned in.''

Settling his hands on his denim-clad hips, Nolan growled, ''She is not penned in.''

''That's apparently how she feels,'' Kathryn snapped. ''And if you don't stop charging around, barking orders, she's going to disappear from your life. If not by marrying Jarrett McMullen, then some other way.''

Before the man could formulate another hateful reply, Kathryn spied Devon and Rick coming from the rear of the store, both of them holding soft-drink cans. The little boy started toward Gray, waving the can dangerously near several racks of delicate silk gowns.

With a grace that belied his size, Gray met the boy midstore and took the can before a spill could occur. ''Whoa, there, partner,'' he said, his tone remarkably free of the acid he had used when speaking to Kathryn. ''Be careful.''

''But Gray, they've got a cake back there this high.'' Eyes wide, Rick held a hand well above his head to illustrate. ''Are Ashley and Jarrett going to have one like that?''

''I doubt it,'' his brother replied, looking grim once more. Hand on the boy's shoulder, Gray turned him toward Devon. ''Now let's thank the nice ladies for the drink and go. I need to get to the office.''

''But where's Ashley?''

With a patience that surprised Kathryn, Gray said, ''Just say thank-you, Rick. Ashley'll be home later.''

Rick said his thanks, and as quickly as they had appeared, the males were gone, leaving two sets of muddy footprints on the light blue carpeting.

"Oh, my," Devon murmured in the sudden, sharp silence that followed. "My, my, my."

Kathryn was familiar with Devon's look and tone. She always looked and sounded this way when she met a man she thought Kathryn should be interested in.

"Get real," Kathryn grated. "The man's a jerk."

Devon was busy peering through the glass door. "A jerk with a fine-looking butt."

"Devon!" Kathryn shot a glance toward the dressing rooms. "His sister is still back there."

"Surely she's used to women ogling her brother. He's gorgeous."

"I didn't notice."

Wheeling from the door, Devon stared at Kathryn. "Didn't notice those blue eyes? That dark hair? Those big, strong shoulders?"

Kathryn had noticed all of that and more, but she wouldn't admit it to Devon. "All I noticed was his insufferable cockiness."

"You could tame that out of him."

"Men like that don't tame," Kathryn said. "I know. I tried it once."

Devon shrugged that off without comment. "He can't be all bad. Did you see how sweet he was to Rick?"

Kathryn turned and headed back to the dressing rooms where Ashley probably needed a hand with the dress. She knew better than to discuss men with Devon. The woman had appointed herself an expert on the subject of whom Kathryn should or shouldn't date.

But Devon wasn't to be deterred. "Rick's a real cutie, too. They could be a great little package deal for some eager woman."

"There may be some eager woman waiting at

home," Kathryn muttered before ducking through the curtained archway that led to the dressing rooms.

Devon's lilting "I didn't see a ring" filtered through the curtains.

Kathryn put the annoying Gray Nolan out of her head and concentrated on his half sister instead. Ashley was still wearing her dream dress, though she was propped on a stool in front of the mirror, the skirt pooled around her like so much frothy whipped cream. Unlike the tears Kathryn had expected, the young woman's unusual tawny eyes were filled with determination. Ashley was petite and delicately pretty, but for the first time, Kathryn saw the resemblance between her and Gray.

"I heard what he said to you about not doing the wedding," Ashley told her. "I'm sorry I made so much trouble for you."

"You didn't," Kathryn soothed.

"I guess you'd like to tell me to take my business elsewhere."

That was exactly what Kathryn wanted. But how could she say that to this anxious young woman? Ashley was engaged to Jarrett McMullen, whose older sister, Paige, had been Kathryn's best friend in college. The McMullens had been of invaluable help when Kathryn moved from Fort Worth to Amarillo and set up her wedding boutique, and their support had continued through the years. If Jarrett was getting married, Kathryn was the only logical choice to coordinate his wedding. She owed that much to his family, and especially to Paige McMullen, who was now living in California. Kathryn wouldn't back off unless Paige or Jarrett's father asked her to.

"Don't worry," Kathryn told Ashley. "I'm sure everything will work out for the best."

"Oh, I'm sure things will work out. Because Jarrett and I are getting married, no matter what Gray says or does. And I'm going to wear this dress." Ashley stood, preening in front of the mirror once more. "I'm just afraid of how much trouble Gray's going to cause along the way."

Kathryn was secretly afraid of the same thing, but she didn't know what she could do to change matters. Gray Nolan was just as stubborn and determined as his sister. The less Kathryn saw of him, the happier she would be. Although in some perverse way, it might be enjoyable to watch him suffer.

"You've got to talk to him some more," Ashley said, interrupting her thoughts.

Kathryn shook her head. "No, Ashley. That's not part of the services I provide."

"Please." Ashley turned and grasped Kathryn's hands. "Please, Miss Seeger. Me and Jarrett really need your help with Gray. He could ruin this for us if you don't. I wouldn't ask if I had anyone else who could talk to him. But we only moved here last year. Gray has some friends back in Oklahoma, but there's not much they can do, I'm afraid. And we don't have any family that we're close to who could talk to him about this. I really need some help."

Even as she protested again, Kathryn could feel herself beginning to waver. It was the same slipping sensation she felt each time one of her brides asked for the impossible.

As Devon often said, Kathryn was a pushover when it came to helping dream weddings come true. She had remade gowns on the nights before weddings, procured doves to release during ceremonies, rented airplanes to paint messages in the sky and once hired an Elvis impersonator to entertain at a reception.

Elvis was easy.

Getting Gray Nolan to approve of this wedding was one miracle Kathryn wasn't sure she could accomplish.

"I'm a jerk."

Late that afternoon, Gray gave voice to his thoughts as he guided his Jeep out of the parking lot of his veterinary office.

On the seat beside him, Rick said, "How come?"

Gray, who hadn't intended to speak aloud, grunted in reply.

But as usual, his eight-year-old brother didn't let him off so easily. "Are you talking about fighting with Ashley?"

"Yeah." Sighing, Gray edged into a stream of evening traffic and looked over at Rick. "I shouldn't have gone barging into that store and made such a ruckus."

Rick considered that for a few solemn minutes, then agreed, "Probably not."

"Your sister's going to be hot about it."

"Maybe we better take home a pizza for dinner. It's her night to cook, I think."

Grinning, Gray ruffled the boy's hair. Rick was always up for pizza. "Good idea."

But as Gray headed toward their favorite pizza parlor, he thought it was going to take a whole lot more than pepperoni with extra cheese to make up with his sister.

He never should have stopped at that boutique this afternoon. Earlier, he had been called to Rick's school for a conference with a counselor, then had to take the boy along on an emergency call at a ranch west of town. Gray had been muddy, tired and on emotional overload from Rick's troubles at school and his worry over Ashley's engagement. When he had seen his sister's Honda Civic parked at the renovated house where the boutique was located, he had seen red. All of a sudden, the wedding he had been denying would happen had become a terrifyingly real possibility. He had reacted without thinking, wheeling in there, tearing inside with mud all over his boots, reading Ashley the riot act, then carrying on with the owner like a no-class bum. Though he was sure Ashley might disagree, such obnoxious behavior wasn't his usual mode of operation.

What had happened to him and Ashley?

Gray had asked himself that question ever since leaving the boutique. As he did paperwork and returned the phone calls that were a routine part of most late afternoons at his large-animal veterinary practice, he had continued to puzzle over his disintegrating relationship with his sister. He was still worrying now, as he picked up the pizza and he and Rick drove through the gathering May twilight toward the little spread north of town where they lived.

The West Texas sky was beautiful, gilded orange, red and purple by the setting sun. But as Gray had expected, the house was dark; Ashley wasn't home. What a change from just a year ago. In Oklahoma, where they had lived before, Ashley or Rick always came charging to the door when he got home, eager to tell him about their days or to hear about his. Now Ashley barely spoke to him unless it was to tell him some new, irritating detail about this ridiculous wedding. More often than not, she wasn't even home.

Maybe if they had stayed in Oklahoma instead of moving, she would be planning for college instead of marriage. Gray had uprooted her whole life by moving them to Amarillo last summer, just before her senior year in high school. Instead of graduating with friends she had known since kindergarten, in three weeks she would receive her diploma with virtual strangers. But the move wasn't really the problem. Ashley had made friends. She was too pleasant and bright for anything otherwise. And she hadn't really seemed too upset about the move at first. With the maturity she used to possess, she had told Gray the chance for him to buy an existing veterinary practice sounded like a great opportunity, and she had felt the change would do Rick good. The youngest member of their family had suffered the most after their mother died. He had some emotional problems and struggled in school. Gray and Ashley had always been united in their protectiveness toward Rick.

Soon after they moved, however, Ashley began resenting most of the suggestions Gray made about everything—from her friends to her schoolwork to the way she dressed. He had never thought of himself as critical, but she acted as if he was an ogre. And after meeting Jarrett McMullen during Christmas break, she had stopped talking to Gray about anything more important than dinner.

Jarrett McMullen. The scourge of Gray's life.

Scowling at the very thought of the tall, handsome young man who had taken over Ashley's life, Gray shepherded Rick into the house and supervised the reheating and serving of the pizza. If only Jarrett McMullen hadn't taken to coming home from Texas Tech in nearby Lubbock every weekend this winter. If only Gray had seen the danger in allowing Ashley to go with some girlfriends to visit the campus. Foolishly, Gray had believed she and her friends were checking out the school. He had been pleased, as it was a good school and not too far from home. Gray had even welcomed the idea that Jarrett was there to look after the girls on their visits. He had actually liked Jarrett. He had never suspected just how serious Jarrett and Ashley were becoming.

Two weeks ago, on a Sunday night, Jarrett had arrived at the house with Ashley. Very earnestly, the young man had asked Gray for her hand in marriage. But needing or wanting his permission was a joke, since Gray's refusal had been met with a "Well, that's too bad, because we're getting married anyway," from Ashley, who had waved that damned ring in his face.

Jarrett had been asked to leave and not come back. Gray had threatened to confiscate Ashley's car keys and lock her in her room. Their home had become an armed camp.

With the tension in this family, Gray mused, it was no wonder Rick was having a more difficult time than usual in controlling his temper and concentrating on his schoolwork. No wonder Gray's fuse was so short that he had barked at that very attractive and very nice lady at the wedding boutique.

Recalling the boutique owner's trim figure, flashing green eyes and raven hair required no effort whatsoever on his part. Nor was it difficult to remember her assertion that his continuing to fight this marriage would only force Ashley further away from him.

Damn it, maybe she was right.

When Gray had gone over to discuss this problem with Jarrett's father, Rex McMullen had advised him not to panic, either. This was May. The wedding was planned for late August. Rex thought a lot could happen between now and then. Rex was giving Jarrett no encouragement about the wedding, nor was he jumping up and down and screaming in protest. Gray wished he could be so certain the kids would see the foolishness of their plans to marry so young.

Frustrated and weary, Gray pushed a half-eaten slice of pizza away from him.

"Aren't you hungry?" Rick asked, having devoured three wedges already.

"Guess not." Restlessly, Gray got up to peer out one of the corner windows that bracketed the kitchen table. He hoped to see Ashley's car turn into the driveway. The family cat, a gray-and-white tabby named Bettina, rubbed against his leg and meowed. Twin beagles, Tiddly and Winks, gave halfhearted barks from their usual positions on either side of Rick's chair. "These animals need to be fed," Gray advised his young brother. "Just like the pony in the barn."

Rick, who had started on his fourth piece of pizza, mumbled, "In a minute."

The counselor had reminded Gray today that Rick needed consistency and discipline. "Feeding them is your responsibility."

Rick finished his meal and with obvious reluctance led the dogs and cat to their dishes in the utility room. Gray cleared the table, reflecting as he did every night that he had to get on with remodeling the ranch house's outdated kitchen. The rest of the house had been spruced up with paint and some plumbing and tile work in the bathrooms before he bought it. This room, as Ashley was so quick to point out every day, was dismal.

Lights from an automobile played across the corner windows just as Gray opened the dishwasher and began to load the dishes that were piled in the sink from last night and this morning. He made sure the car was Ashley's before returning to his task. A car door slammed, followed a few moments later by the door leading from the back porch to the utility room.

Gray heard Ashley greet Rick with a lilting, "Hey, there, Short-stuff, how was school?" He listened as the boy answered, then brother and sister talked for a few minutes before Rick took the dogs and went to finish his chores in the barn. Gray was aware without looking up when Ashley walked into the kitchen and crossed silently to the refrigerator.

Not stopping what he was doing, Gray kept his tone even. "There's pizza if you want it."

"No, thank you." The girl's voice was as cold as the air blowing out of the freezer compartment.

"So you've already eaten?"

"I'm not hungry."

"You need to eat."

At that comment, Ashley slammed the freezer door with such force the magnets holding notes and pictures on the front fell to the floor with a clatter.

Now Gray looked at her, his eyes narrowing.

Ashley looked mad enough to spit fire, as their mother used to say. "Will you just get off my back?" she demanded as she gathered up the fallen items and slapped them back on the refrigerator.

A thousand angry words sprang to Gray's tongue. But he held them back. Ashley stalked away, heading for the doorway that led to the hall. She stopped only when Gray managed a quiet "Ashe, I'm sorry about today." She didn't turn around, so Gray added, "I'm genuinely sorry I embarrassed you at that shop."

After a few wavering moments, Ashley faced him. Her pretty, even features were pale, her chin set at a stubborn angle.

"You look just like Mom when you're really mad," Gray said, trying to smile. "You've looked a lot like her lately."

Her posture relaxing as if she were suddenly weary, Ashley pushed a hand through her heavy blond hair and leaned one shoulder against the arched doorway. "Lately I've had a hard time remembering how she looked."

Gray swallowed, surprised by the sudden burst of grief he felt. "That's not surprising. You were just eleven when she died. You were a little girl."

"But I'm not a little girl now."

Turning away, Gray nodded. "I know that, Ashe. You haven't really been a kid since Mom left me to look after you and Rick. I've had to depend on you a lot, and you've never let me down."

"Then why are you treating me like a baby?"

Again impulsive words threatened to spill out, but Gray bit them back. "Let's not fight, okay? Let's talk." Calmly, he put some pizza on a plate and placed it in the microwave to warm.

He heard Ashley expel a deep breath. "Okay, Gray. I'll be happy to talk, if you'll listen."

When the timer buzzed, he took the pizza from the oven, placed it on the table in front of her and took a seat. "Please sit down and talk to me."

Sliding her hands into the back pockets of her baggy, faded jeans, Ashley moved to the center of the room.

"I love Jarrett. I want to marry him. That's really all there is to say, just as I've told you a million times."

"But why right now?"

"Why not?" she shot back. "Why should we wait?"

"Because he's the first boy you've been serious about, the first boy..." Words failed Gray. He cleared his throat, then made himself look at her and ask the question he dreaded. "He is the first, isn't he?"

"The first boy I ever loved? Yes."

Gray looked at her, eyebrow cocked, hoping she would discern his true meaning. He just couldn't say, *the first boy you've slept with*. It wasn't that he and his sister had never had the birds-and-bees talks. But those had been general discussions, and this was very specific.

Comprehension dawned in Ashley's face. And she laughed. A trilling, high-spirited laugh that had been too long absent from this household. The full-throttle laugh turned to chuckles as she slid into the seat opposite Gray's and began toying with the pizza.

Gray's face grew warm. "What's so funny? It's a perfectly natural question for the person who has raised you to ask."

"It's none of your business."

"I'm not just prying, Ashe. I'm worried about your getting in over your head emotionally."

She looked highly amused and altogether too comfortable discussing the subject at hand. "If I'd wanted to dive in, there have been other boys who were willing." She laughed again, then quieted when he didn't respond. "Gosh, Gray, if you must know, I haven't even taken the plunge with Jarrett."

He was torn between relief and surprise. "So you haven't...and he hasn't..."

"We haven't slept together," Ashley said, putting him out of his misery.

Gray sat still for a moment, carefully weighing the wisdom of his next words. He finally looked his sister straight in the eye. "Maybe you should."

She blinked. "Huh?"

"Maybe you and Jarrett should take the plunge."

She sat back in her chair, gaping at him. "What are you saying?"

"Just that you may be confusing lust with love."

Eyes narrowing, she considered that for a moment. "So, in a world that preaches abstinence, you, my brother, my guardian, are advising sex."

Gray closed his eyes, considering his advice again. Then he nodded.

"You're certifiable," Ashley announced, jerking up and away from the table.

"Wait a minute. You asked me to talk to you, and that's what I'm doing. I certainly wouldn't give you this kind of advice lightly."

"But you're nuts. You think the only reason I want to marry Jarrett is to sleep with him. Just how stupid and shallow do you think I am?"

"Not stupid or shallow at all. Just awfully young and inexperienced."

"I'm so tired of hearing that," Ashley said through clenched teeth. "You're probably plenty experienced, but that doesn't mean you have the slightest concept of the reasons why two people might want to be married."

"We're not discussing me."

"Maybe we should. Because you seem to think every marriage has to turn out like Mom's did."

Gray sighed, not wanting to rehash their sad but true family history.

But Ashley was warming to her subject. "I guess I can see why you might feel pretty pessimistic about marriage, considering how your dad and Mom divorced when you were a baby and she was just nineteen. And then she married and divorced mine and Rick's dad, who stayed until most of Grandfather's money was gone, then left before Rick was even born."

The tremor in Ashley's voice got to Gray. "Stop it. There's no need to go over this."

"But there is," she protested, the sadness in her tone replaced by determination. "You think I'm making the same mistake our parents did. Well, I'm not. I love Jarrett, and he loves me. If anything, Mom's mistakes have made me see exactly what I'm getting into."

Gray didn't want to fall into clichés, but he couldn't resist. "If you love each other so much, can't you wait?"

Ashley groaned and rolled her eyes. "God, can't you do any better than that?"

"I happen to think there's nothing wrong in waiting. In a couple of years, when you and Jarrett have finished school, if you feel the same way, I'll welcome him into the family."

Ashley wasn't buying that. "What you really need to do, Gray, is get a life of your own and let me have mine."

The lid he had slammed down earlier on his anger threatened to blow off. "I have a life."

"Then how come you haven't had a date since we moved?"

"I've been busy. There's the business. And you kids."

Now Ashley's laughter lacked mirth. "Don't use us as an excuse. That's what you did with Gina."

Mention of the woman he had been engaged to marry several years before cut the last tie Gray held on his temper. "We're not talking about Gina, either."

"Well, I want to talk about her," Ashley returned. "Ever since she left, you've been like this bitter old man. More like forty than thirty-one."

"Just because I won't give this crazy wedding my blessing, you say I'm bitter."

"No, I say that because you're so narrow in your views, so set in your ways. The real reason you don't want me to get married is because once I'm out of this house you won't be able to control me."

Her statement hit dangerously close to the accusation the boutique owner had made about his "penning" Ashley in. He didn't want to believe that was true. "I don't want to control you. Hell, if you want to leave and go anywhere you want to college, you have my blessing. I'd rather you do anything other than jump into a young, foolish marriage."

"So you're saying I could handle going thousands of miles away to live on my own, but I'm not mature enough to marry Jarrett and live an hour and half away in Lubbock?"

"You're comparing apples and oranges, Ashe."

"And you're not giving me any credit. Other people say I'm more mature than people twice my age."

"Who says that?"

"Miss Seeger...Kathryn."

"Who?"

"The lady at the shop whose head you tried to take off this afternoon."

"She thinks you're mature?"

"Before you came roaring in, she was telling me what good taste I have, how I seem to know what I want, how decisive I am compared to some of the people she works with on weddings. More mature and more decisive than lots of people years older than me," she said.

Gray snorted in disgust. "She was just trying to sell you that dress."

Indignant, Ashley drew herself up to her full five-feet-four inches of height. "Kathryn is not like that. Jarrett's whole family thinks she's wonderful, and I like her, too. She wouldn't have said I was mature for my age if she didn't mean it."

Gray still had his doubts about Kathryn Seeger's motives in complimenting his sister. But Ashley sure seemed to like her.

"If you want to know the truth," Ashley continued, "I think Kathryn is one of the nicest people I've met since we've moved here. She and I hit it off just like that." She snapped her fingers to illustrate. "And she's known Jarrett's family so long that if she had any doubts about our getting married, I think she would have said so."

What Kathryn Seeger would or wouldn't do was something Gray didn't know. What he did see, however, was that the boutique owner had made a strong impression on Ashley in a short amount of time. And that was what he needed. Someone his hardheaded younger sister would listen to. For it was clearer than ever that she wasn't prepared to listen to him.

Maybe he needed to get this Kathryn Seeger, this

paragon of virtue whom the beloved Jarrett admired so much, on his side.

"What are you thinking?"

Gray shook himself out of his reverie.

Hands on her hips, Ashley was staring at him with suspicion. "You've got a funny look on your face."

He half smiled, plans for soliciting Miss Seeger's help spinning through his head.

Ashley studied him, clearly perplexed. "I don't like that smile. You're easier to deal with when you're yelling at me."

Gray got up. "You sure are hard to please. Does Jarrett know that about you?"

"What are you up to?" Ashley asked again as he started to head outside and check on what was keeping Rick at the barn.

Gray's reply was noncommittal, but he paused at the door and looked back at his sister. "Just one thing, Ashe. About the 'taking the plunge' advice I gave you..."

"Yeah?"

"Forget it, okay? I was desperate. But you've done right by waiting this long. You keep things just the way they are."

She rolled her eyes and made a low sound of disgust.

Gray went outside, hoping she would do as he advised. As he crossed the yard to the barn, he decided he would get rolling on his plan with Kathryn Seeger tomorrow afternoon. He would pay the lovely lady a visit, apologize profusely for his behavior and then beg her to help him. Once upon a time, he'd been told he wasn't without charm. If he remembered how to use that charm, he might be able to convince the boutique owner, *the really pretty boutique owner*, that this wedding was a bad idea and it was her duty to bow out of the plans.

Gray frowned, realizing this was the third or fourth time since leaving the boutique that he had thought about Kathryn Seeger in terms of her attractiveness. Her appeal didn't matter. All that mattered to him right now was putting an end to Ashley's wedding.

As he headed for the boutique late the next afternoon, he kept telling himself that stopping this wedding was all he cared about.

Then he walked inside.

The little bell tinkled over the door.

The feminine laces and satins of the shop closed around him.

A light, yet spicy perfume washed through the air.

And on the raised platform where Ashley had been standing the day before, Kathryn Seeger turned to face him.

She was wearing a simple, sleeveless dress, as black as her hair, so body-hugging that not one curve of her tall, slender frame was left to his imagination.

Not that his imagination clicked off. Instead, his mind kicked into hyperdrive, and left him wondering just how she might look without the dress, with her long strand of pearls resting between her full breasts.

The projected image had a hardening effect on the most masculine region of his body. Then his mouth went dry. His neck began to perspire.

God, Ashley was right.

He really needed to get a life.

Chapter Two

The man who stood unmoving just inside the boutique door was vaguely familiar to Kathryn. At this distance, she couldn't quite see his face. But she liked the rest of him—the long legs and broad shoulders, the straight, sure way he held himself. His lightweight sport coat, well-worn jeans and white polo were the epitome of Texas casual chic for men. As he ambled around the customers Devon was talking with midstore, Kathryn turned, pretending to study herself in the triple mirror. In reality, she let herself appreciate this man's easy, graceful walk.

He moved like a mountain cat, she decided. She turned toward him, glancing first at his scuffed but clean boots. She smiled as her gaze moved up his body and came to rest on his light blue eyes. Recognition struck. Her stomach clenched.

The hunk she was undressing with her eyes was Ashley's brother, the insufferable Gray Nolan.

More shocking, however, was the striptease his eyes were performing on her.

For several heated moments, she stood unmoving on the dais, her gaze locked tight on his. For a woman who prided herself on strict control, Kathryn was having a hard time keeping her pulse in check.

Finally, after he had stepped right up onto the platform with her, he came to a halt. "Hello, Miss Seeger."

Kathryn called upon the social poise she had been taught at her mother's knee. "Mr. Nolan." Then, mindful of all the details the resourceful, matchmaking Devon had told her about this man earlier today, she corrected herself. "I guess it's *Dr.* Nolan."

"Please call me Gray."

She let that pass. "I didn't expect to see you again so soon."

His smile was altogether too appealing as he held out his hand. "I was afraid you'd have a guard at the door to keep me out."

"Well, we haven't seen the need to employ a bouncer." She forced herself not to shiver like a naive virgin when his big, rough-palmed hand closed over hers. "Not yet anyway."

"I came to apologize," he said.

"Really?"

"I regret the scene I made yesterday. And..." Grinning ruefully, he glanced toward the floor, where the imprint of his and Rick's muddy boots hadn't quite disappeared. "I'm also sorry about tracking mud across the carpet. My mama raised me to do better than that."

Something in the way his deep, even tones said the

word "mama" caused a melting sensation inside Kathryn. Lord, she was being a fool.

"I'll be glad to pay the carpet cleaning bill," he continued earnestly.

Kathryn managed to extract her hand from his and waved the offer away. "Good heavens, you have to expect a little dirt on the floor if you're going to do business in West Texas."

"I think you're just being polite."

"My mama taught me to mind my manners, too."

His gaze brushed over her with blatant approval. "Looks like she did a mighty fine job teaching you a lot of things."

Unnerved and yet intrigued by his familiarity, Kathryn stepped back.

Gray Nolan took hold of her arm. "Watch it, now. I wouldn't want you to take a tumble off this platform."

"Thank you," Kathryn said, quickly drawing her arm away. Normally, she hated being crowded by big, overprotective men. Just because she was finding this man's attention disturbingly pleasant was no reason to let down her normal guard. "Was there something else you wanted from me?" She glanced at her watch. "We were just about to close and I'm due at a reception—"

"I won't keep you," Gray said. "Is there some other time when you and I could talk?"

"Talk?"

"About the wedding."

She studied him with suspicion. "You're agreeing to the wedding?"

He looked her straight in the eye, any hint of flirtatious amusement gone from his expression. "Not exactly."

"I think I told you yesterday that I don't interfere in the family feuds of my clients."

"Even when one of the people involved is part of a family you count as close, personal friends?"

"Even then."

"Ashley told me that you've known Jarrett and his family a long time. That you and Jarrett's sister are close."

"Yes, Paige and I are good friends, even though she doesn't live here in Amarillo now. But neither she nor Jarrett's father are creating a big fuss about the wedding."

Indeed, Kathryn had spoken with Rex McMullen this morning. Jarrett and Paige's father said he didn't think interfering would do anything other than speed up the wedding. He also said he thought Ashley Grant was a lovely, mature young woman, and that if Jarrett married her, it might not be the end of the world that Gray Nolan was prophesying. It seemed meeting Ashley had made Jarrett buckle down to his studies. Rex, a wealthy man, also said that if the wedding didn't come off, he would cover any expenses Kathryn might incur. Though she didn't need such an assurance from a friend, Kathryn appreciated his offer. She was running a business after all. Once again, she reminded Gray Nolan just what that business was.

Sighing, he shoved a hand through his wavy, dark hair. His gaze was centered on his boots. "Miss Seeger, I know you have little reason to believe this, but I'm generally a pretty rational guy. But this thing with Ashley..." Taking another deep breath, he lifted a misery-filled gaze to her once again. "I really need your help."

"I don't see what I could do."

"I think she might listen to you."

"As I said yesterday, I hardly know your sister."

"But she likes you." He put out his hand again. "Please, can't you help me?"

Kathryn swallowed hard. She wished he was the same rude cowboy who had barged in here and started giving her orders yesterday. She could resist that man. But this one...

"Kathryn?"

It took her a minute to realize Devon was calling her name. Grateful for the interruption, she wheeled away from Gray Nolan. To her surprise, Kathryn saw that the shop had emptied of the last customers while she had stood talking to him.

"You need me?" Kathryn asked her associate as she stepped down from the platform.

Devon was shrugging into a pink linen jacket whose color complemented her curly chestnut hair. Her brown eyes were fairly dancing with mischief. "I'm sorry, Kathryn. I'm not going to be able to go to that cocktail party with you."

"Why not?"

"Well..." The shorter woman fluttered her long lashes, clearly improvising. "I have a terrible headache."

"Since when?"

"Oh." Devon shifted her gaze past Kathryn, to Gray Nolan. "Since about fifteen minutes ago."

Kathryn glared at her.

"I'm awfully sorry." Devon's lips trembled, no doubt because she was struggling not to laugh.

"I'll make you sorry," Kathryn whispered.

Devon ignored her and focused her attention on Gray. "Dr. Nolan, are you busy tonight?"

Kathryn, who refused to turn around, felt, rather than saw him hesitate.

He cleared his throat. "Well, no—"

"Good," Devon cut in brightly. "I promised to go to this cocktail party with Kathryn tonight. But now I'm not feeling well, and she just hates going to these things by herself. Could you stand in for me?"

Kathryn closed her eyes and thanked God there wasn't a loaded weapon nearby. Then she whipped around to face Gray before he could reply to Devon. "This isn't necessary," she said. "I don't need an escort, of course."

The glance he swept over her was even, measured, undecipherable. "I'd like to go."

"Then you're all set," Devon interjected before Kathryn could protest again. And like a petite, pink tornado, she tore out of the shop.

Sighing, Kathryn darted a glance at the male beside her. "I'm sorry about that."

"Why? Don't you want me to go?"

"No...I mean, that's not it..."

"Then what?"

She thought about explaining to him that Devon saw every single man as a potential mate for Kathryn. Devon had called upon all her resources last night to gather information on Gray. Thanks to Devon, Kathryn now knew he was in his early thirties, just four years out of vet school. He'd had custody of Ashley and Rick ever since their mother died some seven years ago, and had worked his way through school while taking care of his siblings. Devon said she had it on good authority from her aunt, who lived next door to the best friend of Gray's office manager, that Gray was a terrifically nice guy.

And he was single. Unattached. Uninvolved. Available.

Those descriptive words were really all the recommendation Devon needed. His showing up here today had merely played into her matchmaking little hands. Kathryn only wished her employee would spin some romantic schemes for herself, instead of meddling in Kathryn's life.

"Is there a problem?" Gray asked.

Kathryn just shook her head. How could she explain Devon to him when she honestly didn't understand the diminutive young woman herself?

"I'm just afraid you might be bored by this reception."

"Where is it?"

"At a new art gallery."

He lifted an eyebrow. "You don't think veterinarians can appreciate art?"

"Of course you can," she said, irritated that anyone would think her so narrow-minded. "But occasions like this are work for me. In addition to the weddings we do, we sell lots of special-occasion dresses, and we cater all kinds of parties. So I try to stay up on the social scene in town."

"Why aren't you catering this party?"

She smiled. "That's what I'm going to find out."

Despite her delicate looks, Gray was struck by the feeling that this woman was a real competitor. He grinned back. "Maybe I can scout around, find out what they paid for the cocktail wienies."

She laughed. "We won't stay long, I promise."

"It's no problem," Gray said as she excused herself to get her purse from her office. He wasn't lying. Even if he didn't win her help with Ashley, there was nothing he minded about escorting this woman anywhere.

* * *

He didn't like the party nearly as much as her, however.

Located in what was once a drugstore in the historic Old San Jacinto area of Amarillo, the new art gallery's exposed brick walls featured neon sculptures and metal wall hangings and boldly colored canvases that Gray had a difficult time defining as art. He liked his paintings with people and trees and other recognizable objects in them. But that wasn't really what bothered him. It was the way some of the party guests studied him with a mixture of curiosity and disapproval.

He had never felt this way in Amarillo before. From what he had been able to determine, blue jeans were supposed to go everywhere these days. Even if they didn't, he rarely gave a damn about what he wore as long as he was presentable. But from the way the women—and some of the men—at the reception studied him, he was beginning to think he had committed a fashion crime. Or maybe it wasn't what he was wearing at all. Maybe they could sense what he thought of the art, of their phony laughter and preening demeanor. This was an aspect of Amarillo that Gray hadn't known about until now, a sidebar to the stockyards, cowboys and Texas-size steaks that had made the place famous. And he was probably embarrassing Kathryn Seeger in front of her fancy friends.

She had been drawn from his side from the moment they arrived, swallowed up by a group of men and women whose clothes and manner bore the same aura of sophistication as hers. In that way, and that way only, Kathryn reminded Gray of Gina, the woman he had almost married. The comparison didn't evoke many pleasant memories for him.

Gina had been beautiful and wealthy. She'd brought a do-gooder zeal to her relationships with him and the kids. But she broke their engagement only weeks before the wedding date, citing his "emotional distancing" as the reason. Not long after, she married a man as rich as she, a man without Gray's family complications. Gray was convinced he and his family had been no more than a rich girl's charity project.

Up in the loft that overlooked the gallery's main floor, Gray stood at the railing and watched Kathryn break away from a circle of sleekly dressed and coiffed young patrons. She looked up at him as if she had been aware of his scrutiny all along. She started up the stairs, her gaze remaining on his. A slow smile spread across her face as she cleared the steps and came across the loft toward him. Even as Gray reminded himself of his mistakes with Gina, his interest in Kathryn deepened.

"Are you bored yet?" she whispered once she had reached his side.

"Not if you're not."

"Your mama did raise a well-mannered boy, didn't she?"

"I told you so." With his half-empty wineglass, Gray pointed toward the painting he had been puzzling over for the past half hour. "For instance, that looks like nothing more than a series of stop signs, but I've refrained from saying so."

Kathryn studied the painting, as well. She cocked her head to the side, her silky black hair swinging forward to curl against the pale skin of her neck. Gray found that sight much more artful than any painting in the place.

"You know what?" she said finally. "I think that painting really is just a series of stop signs."

"But I'm sure it has some deeper, more symbolic meaning."

"Oh, no doubt," Kathryn concurred. The sparkle in her eyes belied her serious tone.

Gray chuckled. She did, too. They laughed harder, louder perhaps than was proper. He sensed others turning to look at them, yet he didn't care. He liked hearing her laugh, liked looking at her and having her look at him. He wondered if she could feel the thread of tension building between them. He wanted to go someplace where they could talk. Ashley was with Rick, so Gray had time for this, time to spend with Kathryn Seeger.

Slowly, he set his glass down on a nearby table. "Are you ready to get out of here?"

She nodded in answer, her eyes still shining.

He steered her toward the stairs.

"Kathryn? Kathryn, dear, do you have just a moment for me?"

Gray turned to see a pretty, silver-haired woman calling to Kathryn from across the loft.

"She's been a good customer," Kathryn murmured to him. "This'll just take a minute." She left him standing near the top of the stairs and went to meet the woman.

Trying not to betray his impatience, Gray let his gaze drift idly over the crowd. He was soon aware of the intense regard of a blonde near the bar. She was tall, with legs that went on forever, and her tight little red dress made Kathryn's slinky black number seem downright Victorian. The blonde was sipping a drink and looking at Gray with blatant invitation in her eyes.

He looked away. He wasn't interested. He was here with someone who made her look cheap, someone who had lit an unexpected spark inside him. He thought he might want to see where that might lead.

Kathryn appeared at his side again with a bright smile. "Are you ready?"

As they started down the stairs, the lady in red edged past them and turned with a smile, blocking their progress. On closer observation, she was even harder-looking than from a distance. She greeted Kathryn while her gaze slipped over Gray.

Kathryn said hello and, with an amused little smile, introduced Gray to Miss Emmaline Marsh.

"So where are you two going?" the woman purred in a husky drawl Gray was sure some men found sexy. "If it's to another party, I'd love to tag along."

"No other party," Kathryn told her. "Sorry, Emmaline."

"Then how about a drink somewhere?" she suggested, still looking only at Gray.

"Can't do it," he replied.

Miss Marsh pouted her perfectly drawn red lips. "Why not?"

Irritated, he took Kathryn's hand and finally returned the blonde's intense regard. "We have urgent personal business. *Alone.*"

Kathryn made a soft sound of protest, but Gray held her tightly to his side.

The blonde grinned knowingly and arched one thin, sculptured eyebrow. "My, my, Kathryn. You're walking on the wild side with this cowboy. Call me if you need help." Then she breezed off down the steps, no doubt in search of more congenial prey.

Gray was still for a moment, wishing he hadn't said anything more than hello to the blonde. She reminded him of his ex-fiancée's so-called friends. They had played nice-nice, but ogled him like a prize bull on the auction block, propositioning him on more than one occasion when Gina's back was turned. They had always made him feel that Gina was lowering herself to be with him.

Beside him, Kathryn cleared her throat. "Are we going or not?"

"Going. Definitely."

Once outside in the warm May air, as they walked down the sidewalk to where he had parked his Jeep, he reached up to loosen a nonexistent, restricting tie. Kathryn laughed.

"What's so funny?" Gray asked.

"You and Miss Emmaline Marsh. I doubt many men brush her off so easily."

"She made me want to puke."

"Oh, she's a predator. And a terrible gossip. I'm sure she'll tell everyone about my new lover."

Gray drew to a halt. "Do you care what she says? Does it bother you?"

Kathryn stopped, as well, and turned to face him. "Excuse me?"

"Are you embarrassed that I gave the impression we were together?"

"No."

Not sure he believed her, he grunted a reply and started forward again. Kathryn stayed put, however, forcing him to pause.

She crossed her arms. "Other than Ashley and Jarrett's wedding, have you got some sort of problem with me, Dr. Nolan?"

"No."

"Then why do you keep insulting me?"

He blinked. "What do you mean?"

"Earlier, you assumed that I would think a veterinarian wouldn't be interested in art. Now, you assume I would care what someone like Emmaline Marsh thinks or says about me. Why, the woman's a sybarite, someone who—"

Irritation crackling through him, he stopped her explanation. "I know what the word means, Miss Seeger. A sybarite is a pleasure seeker. But by using such a word, then trying to explain it, maybe you were talking down to me, trying to make me look and feel foolish."

"I wasn't talking down," she retorted, clearly affronted. "I was just talking, maybe talking too much. That's what I do when someone annoys me."

He executed an admittedly smart-alecky salute. "Pardon me for annoying you, ma'am."

"Now that's just what I mean. You're trying to make out that I'm some sort of snob. And I don't know why in the world you'd think that. I'm just a working woman, a shop owner. For God's sake, you're a doctor."

"A vet."

"Are you ashamed of that or something?"

"Hell no. I worked damned hard to get where I am."

"I did, too." She placed fisted hands on her hips. "So why are you acting like I'm some kind of prima donna?"

"I'm not sure," he shot back.

"You don't even know me."

"You're right."

"So stop making assumptions."

"All right."

"And take me somewhere for dinner."

Her quick change of subject gave him pause. The

soft smile that curved her lips rocked him back on his heels.

"I'm hungry," she said as casually as if they hadn't just had a near argument. "The hors d'oeuvres in there weren't fit to eat."

He cleared his throat. "I'm sure yours would have been great."

"You're damn straight." She held out her hand for his. "Now let's go eat. I could really go for a burger."

He grinned, a fabulous grin, and took her hand, and inside Kathryn a voice screamed, *What are you doing?*

She had no idea. All she was certain of was that it had been a long, long time since she had felt a man watch her the way Gray Nolan had watched her at the cocktail party. When she had looked up and seen him standing by the loft railing, studying her, she had felt a current between them as strong as a riptide. His gaze had drawn her up those stairs and to his side. When he had asked if she wanted to leave, all sorts of naughty thoughts had danced through her head. Those thoughts remained as she climbed into his Jeep and they drove to a popular restaurant and saloon.

Kathryn tried to get hold of herself. The man was arrogant; she had witnessed that yesterday. He had a chip on his shoulder, as well; she had seen proof of that just a few minutes ago. But for all those strikes against him, he was disturbingly sexy and surprisingly appealing; she felt that right now, as they squeezed into a corner booth in a bar crowded with Friday night revelers. The restaurant side of the establishment was full, but they'd been told they could order dinner here.

"Sure this is okay?" Gray asked, his gaze sweeping around the room after they had ordered burgers and a couple of beers.

"They have the best burgers in town."

"So I've heard."

"You've never been here?"

"I wouldn't have thought you had."

She tsk-tsked. "There you go again, making assumptions."

He looked shamefaced. "I'm sorry. You just don't look…"

She completed his statement. "I just don't look like a woman who enjoys noisy bars or a good beer."

"No, you don't."

"How does someone like that look?"

He nodded toward a group of women who were wearing tight jeans and low-cut blouses and flirting outrageously with a group of young studs.

Kathryn laughed. "Dr. Nolan—"

"I wish you'd stop calling me that."

"All right. *Gray.* You've got to stop making such generalizations. People will think you don't get out much."

"I don't," he admitted with a wry smile just as the waitress appeared with their drinks.

"Why don't you get out?" Kathryn asked.

He shrugged. "I've been busy getting my practice off the ground."

"You bought old Doc Tester's practice."

"Right."

"And you're exclusively a large-animal vet."

"I guess Ashley told you that."

Kathryn shook her head. "I'm afraid your sister didn't have much to say about you. Not much that was nice anyway."

He sat forward, frowning down at the scarred

wooden table. "I wish Ashley and I could work this out."

Kathryn murmured something noncommittal and took a sip of her beer as she gazed around the bar.

"Are you going to help me with Ashe?"

She met his intense gaze once more. "Gray, I think I've made it clear I'm not willing to get in the middle of this."

"I just need someone to talk to her sensibly about the realities of what she and Jarrett are planning." He went on to explain that he had tried to enlist Jarrett's father's help, but to no avail.

Kathryn thought Rex McMullen was handling this engagement the right way, but she didn't say that. "Gray, surely there's someone else who can talk to Ashley. A teacher, perhaps."

He shook his head. "Ashley had so many credits heading into her senior year that she's basically floated through these final classes. She hasn't said much about getting close to any teachers. As for anyone else, once she met Jarrett just about everyone else disappeared from her life. She has some girlfriends, but from what I've seen they think her marrying Jarrett is a great idea." He sighed and tossed back nearly half his beer.

Though Kathryn knew she was making a mistake, she decided to once again offer the advice she had given him before. "I think you should back off."

Gray's eyes narrowed. "You said that yesterday."

"It's been my experience that young women who think they're in love have to find their own way through these things."

"Your experience? You mean from working with brides at your shop?"

"That and..." Kathryn paused. There was really no

reason to say anything more, anything personal. Except that she knew firsthand how a clash of wills could drive a wedge through a family. From the little she knew about Gray Nolan and his siblings, she figured it would be a shame if anything happened to separate them at this point. "I know about young brides," she told Gray, "because I was just eighteen when I got married."

He sat up, brow furrowing. "You're married?"

"Divorced. The marriage only lasted about eighteen months."

Gray reached out, lightly touching her forearm that rested on the table. "So you do know what a mistake Ashley is making."

"I didn't say that."

"But teenage marriages—"

"Sometimes succeed," Kathryn cut in. "From what I've seen, Ashley is way more mature than I was. And Jarrett is nothing like my ex, Darren."

"How is he different?"

Kathryn shifted uneasily in her seat. She didn't think about her young ex-husband often, hadn't seen him since the day she had finally walked out of the tiny apartment they had shared. Like most of the bad memories in her life, she resisted pulling those that involved Darren out for frequent examination.

"I don't mean to pry."

Gray's deep voice interrupted her thoughts. He was looking at her with concern, making her wonder what kind of feelings her expression had revealed.

Making her tone as neutral as possible, she said, "You're not prying. I'm the one who brought Darren up."

"You looked upset."

She made a face. "It's never easy to think about our failures, is it?"

"No," Gray agreed, looking pensive.

Kathryn sighed. "And my marriage was a spectacular failure. From the start. I married Darren for all the wrong reasons, mainly because my mother hated him."

"Why was that?"

"She thought he was crude and lazy."

"Was he?"

"Yeah."

"So you'd have been better off if she had stopped the wedding."

"I'd have been better off if she had left me alone to see what a loser he was on my own, before we got married."

"You really think you might have seen the light?"

"I thought I was in love," she said, wistfully recalling that innocent time. "So perhaps nothing would have stopped my marrying him. But I might have waited a little while if my mother hadn't kept pulling at me and putting him down. She forced me into a position where I had to defend him. Because of that, I started thinking he was better than he was."

"And you blamed your mother?"

The myriad of feelings Kathryn had for her mother involved some blame, some guilt and a whole lot of bitterness, but that was one personal story she wasn't about to get into tonight. Thankfully, the burgers and fries she and Gray had ordered arrived before their conversation could push further in that direction.

They dug into their meals, their companionable exchanges having to do with the food, the music and the crowd.

Then, abruptly, Gray said, "You think I'm forcing

Ashley to choose Jarrett, just as your mother forced you into choosing your ex.''

Kathryn sighed. She had hoped this subject was closed. ''Ashley's situation is different from mine. Like I said, Jarrett isn't a manipulative bully like Darren was.''

Gray's gaze sharpened. ''Your husband was a bully?''

She shrugged. ''He liked playing control games.''

''And he hurt you.'' Gray's blunt tone put a world of meaning in the word ''hurt.'' Meanings that fit.

Kathryn didn't like the way this man seemed able to read beneath the surface of her words. She worked hard to keep her expression blank. ''Darren had a lot of anger he didn't know what to do with.''

There was a dangerous glint in Gray's eyes. ''So he took it out on you?''

Kathryn bit her lip, looking away. This was the reason she would have been better off not getting into her private history. She didn't want this man, or anyone else, giving her sympathy or pity. Maybe she could lay part of the blame for her young and painful marriage at her mother's feet and part of the blame on Darren's angry nature. But in the end, it had been Kathryn's decision to marry him. Just as it had been her decision to walk away. There was no reason to make a drama out of a situation that had been over and done with for a long time.

''Kathryn?''

With reluctance, she glanced back at Gray.

''We don't know each other very well,'' he said, so quietly she had to lean forward to hear him. ''But I'm sure you didn't deserve whatever your ex did to you.''

She tried to brush it off. ''No one deserves to be

hurt. But we were both so young. We both made mistakes—''

"Don't do that."

The intensity of his tone startled her. "What?"

"Don't make excuses for his being an abusive jerk."

She bristled. "I've never made excuses for anything about my marriage."

Gray looked ready to say something more, then relaxed his tense shoulders, contrition softening his sharpened features. "I'm sorry, Kathryn."

"It's okay."

"No, it isn't. I shouldn't be commenting on a situation I don't know much about. But those guys who take their frustrations out on women get to me."

Kathryn accepted his apology. She chewed thoughtfully on a French fry before saying, "Maybe I'm the one who's out of line now, but it sounds as if you've met up with one of 'those guys' before."

Gray's answer was evasive. "Let's just say that from what I've seen, marriage can bring out the worst in some people."

"What a pessimistic outlook."

"I call 'em as I see 'em."

"And you see marriage as all wrong."

He hesitated. "I didn't say that."

"When would it be right?"

"When two people are ready for the responsibilities and the inevitable problems."

"Inevitable problems," she echoed. "My, but that sounds romantic."

"Once you get past the wedding, marriage doesn't look all that romantic to me."

"You must have some interesting married acquaintances." Kathryn grinned as she pushed her plate aside and reached for her beer.

Defensively, Gray said, "Are you in any hurry to get married again?"

She had to admit she wasn't, but she added, "That doesn't mean I don't believe marriage can work, that it can't be romantic and special. I've seen it happen."

"Your parents?"

Thinking of her parents' distant relationship, Kathryn said, "No, they aren't especially happy."

"But they're still married."

"At this point, I believe they'd both feel a divorce would be inconvenient."

"Sounds chilly," Gray murmured. "A great advertisement for matrimony."

"Yes, but they're not the only married people I know," Kathryn retorted. "I know lots of happy couples. I'm in the wedding business, remember?"

He looked glum again. "How could I forget?"

Impulsively, Kathryn reached out and touched his hand. "Don't worry so much about Ashley. No matter what you think now, I believe Jarrett is an exceptional young man. I think she's special, too."

"She is," he agreed. "She's smart and ambitious. She could be anything she wants."

"If that's true, then even if she does get married, nothing can stop her from reaching her potential."

"But marrying so young will make it harder."

"Or being with someone she really loves might make it easier."

He started a protest, then a smile teased one corner of his mouth. "You know something? I think I'm beginning to see how you've built such a successful business. You have a calming effect on people."

"It helps to remain composed when you're dealing with weddings."

He turned his hand so that their palms were joined. Lightly, he ran his thumb along hers. His touch was pleasing, as pleasant as the contrast between his broad, tanned hand and her slender, pale fingers. The composure Kathryn had just bragged about threatened to unravel. But pulling away was the last thing she wanted to do.

"This has been nice," he murmured.

"Very."

"Not what I expected."

"No, not at all what I expected, either."

At that, his fingers tightened on hers.

Kathryn had dated many men since her divorce. She had sat in other dark corners, holding hands and gazing into another's eyes. But the vast majority of those men had turned into one-date wonders. Devon said she was scared of ending up in another bad relationship. It was true Kathryn wasn't interested in marriage, but she wouldn't mind some companionship. But even if she wasn't looking for a permanent partner, Kathryn did want a man who could strike a chord of magic inside her.

That chord was sounding loud and clear right now. With Gray.

"Kathryn," he murmured in his deep, resonant voice.

Unmoving, she waited for whatever he planned to say, content for the moment just to look at him. At his dark hair, cut short on the sides and in back, waving back from his forehead. At his winged eyebrows, strong nose and well-shaped lips. At the faint stubble along his squared jaw. Without being model perfect,

Gray Nolan was handsome. Outdoorsy. Strong. Supremely masculine.

But Kathryn had dated other handsome men. With Gray there was something more. Maybe it was his desire to protect his sister, or the patient way he had spoken to his young brother, or the way he had come to apologize to her for his outburst in her shop. He had dedicated a large portion of his adult life to raising his half siblings. Not everyone would or could have done that. He was decent, Kathryn thought. Bone-deep honest. A man who cared. A rare man in a world of me-first individualists.

She was so consumed by thoughts of him that she didn't realize when his attention slipped from her. She was caught completely off guard when he jumped to his feet and strode away.

Kathryn blinked, then spun around to watch him push through the crowd and stop at a table across the bar. Through the shifting throng of people, she saw him haul a young man out of his seat.

The young man was Jarrett. Ashley was with him.

And for someone who kept saying she wasn't getting involved in this family fracas, Kathryn moved across the room with lightning speed. She reached Gray's side just in time to hear him demand of his sister, "What in the hell are you doing here?"

The other young men at the table, three tall, beefy specimens in all, jumped to their feet, but Gray was intent on Jarrett, whom he still held by the shirtfront. Jarrett, to his credit, was holding up his hands, not resisting. Ashley, surrounded by several other young women, was angrily demanding that Gray back off.

But it was Kathryn who managed to separate the two

males and quell the other young men's threatening motions with a sharp glance of her own.

"What's the matter?" she asked of Gray.

He jabbed a finger in Ashley's direction. "She's supposed to be home. With Rick."

"There was this party," Ashley said, nervousness warring with defiance in her expression. "Jarrett and I just wanted to stop by, to say goodbye to a friend who's leaving for the summer." She nodded toward one of the young men.

Kathryn frowned, wondering what about this situation had Gray so upset.

"Where's Rick?" he demanded.

Ashley hesitated. "He's at a friend's."

"A friend I know?"

"No, but—"

"Where is he?"

Jarrett spoke up. "It's no big deal, Gray. Rick's fine."

This time, Gray's question was a roar. "Where is he?"

Ashley stuttered out a name and directions to a house not far from the bar.

Gray's glare, which was leveled at Ashley, was pure ice, sharp enough to cut. He wouldn't even look at Jarrett. "I hope to hell he's okay," he grated as he spun away.

Ashley, who was trembling and near tears, said, "Kathryn, Rick is with the mother of a friend of mine. Gray's just overreacting, the same way he overreacts about everything."

But Kathryn had to believe there was some reason why Gray would be this upset. Digging in her purse, she found money, thrust it at Jarrett and told him to pay for her and Gray's dinners. Then she pushed through the crowd and caught up with Gray outside, near his Jeep. She climbed in beside him, and they sped away.

Gray finally spoke as he wove through downtown streets toward a residential section. "Maybe now you see what I'm talking about, Kathryn."

"What?"

"This shows how immature Ashley and Jarrett are. Ashley didn't used to be this way. Before Jarrett McMullen, she never would have dreamed of leaving her brother with someone I don't know."

"I'm sure she wouldn't intentionally put Rick in danger. She said a friend's mother is baby-sitting."

Gray snorted in disgust, and the Jeep's brakes squealed as he drew to a halt in front of a shabby frame house.

As Kathryn followed him up a cracked concrete walk littered with children's toys, she felt her trepidation rising. The door was opened by an older woman, who reacted to Gray's sharp question about Rick by stepping back. From her vantage point, Kathryn could see that the boy was sitting on the floor, contentedly playing a video game with another child. Gray's worries had been ill-founded.

Gray's face was full of raw relief, however. He strode into the room and pulled the surprised-looking boy up and into his arms.

This man's fiercely open love for his younger brother touched Kathryn. Raised by remote and eminently proper parents, she had once yearned for this kind of affection. Maybe that yearning was another reason she had married young; she had been seeking warmth and closeness. The painful failure of her marriage had ended that search for good.

And yet, as she watched Gray hug a wiggling and protesting Rick, she felt a renewal of hope. She fought that rebirth in the way she had taught herself to fight all strong emotions. She had learned the hard way that intense feelings meant a loss of control. Intensity, however, had been the byword ever since Gray had stormed into her shop, wearing his muddy boots.

So she should dismiss him, the same way she usually dismissed the men she met who showed an interest.

She knew that, knew it well. She repeated that instruction to herself all the way back to her shop.

So why in the hell did she insist on Gray bringing Rick up to her apartment for a bite to eat?

Chapter Three

Kathryn lived over her shop in a decorator's dream of an apartment. With white carpeting, pale blue-and-gold floral and striped upholstery and the sort of fragile, feminine doodads that little boys are destined to destroy.

Gray feared his brother and this apartment were on a collision course. He tried to leave, but Kathryn would have none of that. On the ride over, Rick had claimed, with normal eight-year-old fervor, to be starving to death. Kathryn had lured him up to her place with the promise of a sandwich and milk shake. Gray had acquiesced rather than risk one of the boy's tantrums. He figured there had been enough excitement for one evening.

At any rate, Gray wasn't too anxious to go home, where he would no doubt be waiting a long time for Ashley and Jarrett to show up. He wasn't sure what he was going to say to his sister and her boyfriend about tonight's events, but he knew it wouldn't be a pleasant discussion.

So now Rick and Kathryn were in her sparkling white kitchen getting a snack, while Gray stood in the living room, praying nothing would be destroyed.

Kathryn's perfect apartment was symbolic of the reason why Gray couldn't, as Ashley had urged, get a life. Gray's life was much too messy to fit with Kathryn's serene world. With anyone's world, for that matter.

For all of his days, Gray had been contending with messy predicaments. An absent father. A restless mother. A mercenary and selfish stepfather. And then Ashley and Rick. Taking charge was second nature to him. Only one place—at his late grandfather's farm— had he ever felt carefree and easy. But that had been years ago. Now he was burdened, and that didn't mesh with romance. A man needed to be unencumbered if he wanted to date someone. And forget marriage. He had learned with Gina that the sort of ready-made family he presented was much more than any woman wanted.

"You're frowning. Headache?"

He turned to find Kathryn coming toward him with a glass in each hand. "Where's Rick?" he asked.

"Eating at the dinette table. I've got one of those little countertop TVs in the kitchen. He's watching the cartoon cable channel."

With a relieved sigh, Gray took the soft drink she offered. "Just don't let him anywhere near this carpet with food or drink."

"He can't be that messy."

"Sometimes I find food on the walls, Kathryn."

Laughing, she gestured for Gray to take a seat on a

blue-and-white-striped overstuffed sofa. "If he's really that active, you better sit down and take a load off while he's occupied."

"I should just take him home," Gray said, even though he sighed with pleasure as the couch's comfortable cushions gave relief to his tired muscles.

While Gray tried not to admire her long, shapely legs, Kathryn kicked off her black sandals and curled into the sofa's opposite corner. She tugged the black dress to her knees, where it wouldn't quite stay. Gray looked away, his throat suddenly dry. God, he had always been a sucker for pretty legs.

Several moments passed before Kathryn cleared her throat and said, "Rick was hungry, and this is probably just as quick as driving through some fast-food place. I didn't mind getting him a snack."

"But he's had a long day."

Kathryn set her drink on the low, marble-topped table at her elbow. A line appeared between her shapely eyebrows. "Can I ask you something about Rick?"

"Sure."

She glanced toward the kitchen, from which a cartoon soundtrack and boyish laughter were emanating. She lowered her voice. "Is there some sort of problem with him?" At Gray's frown, Kathryn hastened to add, "He acts like every other little boy I know, but you seem…" She bit her lip as if she feared she had said too much.

"Overprotective?" Gray supplied wryly.

"Sort of."

Gray took a long sip of his cola, wondering exactly how to answer.

"Take this evening, for example," Kathryn continued. "I can understand that if you left Ashley in charge of Rick, you weren't too excited to see that she had passed that responsibility off to someone else in order to go out with Jarrett. We all know how you feel about Jarrett. But the baby-sitter turned out to be a nice, responsible grandmotherly type, didn't she?''

"That's how it looked."

"And as I said before, Ashley wouldn't place Rick in danger, would she?"

"Not intentionally." Gray set his own glass on the coffee table and sat forward, elbows on his knees, hands clasped. "The problem is that he's not easy to predict."

Again Kathryn glanced toward the kitchen. "What do you mean?"

"Rick's very smart, curious, a bright kid. But he's also very emotional. He gets upset easily and doesn't always deal with those emotions appropriately. New situations and places are sometimes hard for him."

Kathryn looked doubtful. "He was pretty open with me yesterday and then again tonight, and he was having a great time at the baby-sitter's house."

"But it could have just as easily gone the other way. He needs a lot of structure, a lot of security. He's not always great with strangers. That's something Ashley used to understand." Fighting back a wave of temper, Gray focused on the crystal bowl filled with cobalt blue eggs that rested on the coffee table. "Before Jarrett, Ashley used to think a little more clearly."

When Kathryn remained silent, he glanced up. She had folded her arms across her middle and was studying him thoughtfully.

"You think I'm being too protective," he said, easing back against the cushions again.

She shook her head. "I wouldn't presume to tell you

how a child I barely know should be handled. It's just that…"

"What?" Gray prompted, genuinely interested in hearing her take on the situation.

"Maybe Ashley sees something new in Rick. Maybe she thinks he can handle some situations that you don't."

Gray refused to see that as a possibility. "She's only concerned with herself these days."

"So unusual for an eighteen-year-old," Kathryn murmured, with more than a touch of sarcasm.

"She didn't used to be so typical."

"Which disappoints you terribly."

He was startled by the dry observation. "I guess you think I'm as hard on Ashley as I am protective of Rick."

Kathryn raised a protesting hand. "Oh, goodness, Gray, I've got no business sitting here criticizing you. From what I can see, you've done pretty darn good with both Rick and Ashley."

Now it was his turn to be sarcastic. "I've moved them both to a new place where she's getting married at eighteen, and he's having to adjust to new friends, a new school and a new environment. I've done so well, haven't I?"

"You're being hard on yourself. There are people who would have just walked away from the kids."

"Don't think I haven't been tempted."

"But you stayed. That's what counts."

Gray shrugged, uncomfortable with her praise. He had simply done what he had to do to take care of his family. He didn't see it as any big deal. "The only thing I ever tried to do was make both of them feel secure. It's been hardest with Rick. He barely remembers Mom." He didn't mention Rick's father because in Gray's opinion the man barely counted.

"But you've always been there."

"Sometimes I'm not so great. Ask Ashley."

"When this present crisis passes, I bet she'll give you rave reviews."

"I'd like to believe that."

"I'll check back with her in about five years."

Groaning, he sat up. "I have to wait a whole half a decade?"

"At least. From what I recall, it was at least five years after I was eighteen that I actually became human again." Kathryn smiled, that radiant face-lighting smile Gray thought he could get used to.

Only he had no business getting used to anything about her. They had nothing in common. So what if they traded some longing looks back at that bar tonight? So what if he still remembered how soft and smooth her hand felt in his? As was usual, one of his family crises had intruded before they did more than hold hands. He should be grateful.

Standing abruptly, he said, "We should be on our way."

She looked disappointed. "It's barely nine-thirty."

"And well past Rick's bedtime."

From another room came a protest. "Oh, come on, Gray. It's Friday night."

Gray turned to see his mischievous little brother peeking around the corner of the kitchen doorway.

"All through?" Kathryn asked him.

With his customary energy, Rick came bounding into the room. While Gray cautioned him to be careful, the boy set about examining the living room and its many intriguing objects, directing dozens of rapid-fire questions at a patiently answering Kathryn. Rick finally stopped in front of an ivory pedestal, upon which rested a beautiful glass globe. Lit from within, the orb was an intricate, eye-catching piece.

"Wow," Rick said as his shining, wide eyes rested on the globe. His grubby, little boy's hands reached out immediately.

Gray was beside him in a flash. "Don't touch it."

"It's okay." Kathryn lifted the globe in its golden base from the pedestal and then knelt next to Rick, holding it out for him to look at.

"I'm not sure that's such a good idea," Gray said as Rick's hands closed on the delicate-looking glass.

But Kathryn was not to be deterred. "I'll hold it, too."

Rick was studying the ball with the seriousness of a surgeon examining a patient. "I've never seen a globe like this."

"It came from France," Kathryn told him. "My grandmother brought it home from a trip and gave it to me when I was about your age."

"France is in Europe," Rick said, pointing to the continent outlined on the glass.

"Sure is."

"Does your grandmother live there?"

"No, but she traveled a lot."

"Where is she now?"

Kathryn's expression grew pensive. "She died when I was ten."

Rick nodded, tearing his gaze from the globe to look at her. "My mother's dead."

Keeping one hand on the globe, Kathryn laid her other hand on the boy's shoulder, squeezing gently. Gray noticed that she looked straight at Rick. Gray was impressed. He had seen lots of adults who didn't bother to make eye contact with kids.

Kathryn nodded at the globe again. "Every time my grandmother went on a trip, she brought me back a gift. But this was my most favorite, because it helped me keep up with the places where she went."

"It's cool," Rick said, turning the globe so that the United States faced him. He pointed to Texas. "Here's where we are."

"What grade are you in?" Kathryn asked.

"Third."

"You must get good marks in geography."

Rick shrugged. "That's the easy stuff. It's fractions I don't get."

"Neither do I," Kathryn said, laughing as she started to rise and put the globe back on the pedestal.

"Can I hold it a minute more?" Rick asked.

Before Kathryn could reply, Gray stepped in. No way was he going to take a chance on Rick turning an object of obvious value, sentimental and otherwise, into dust. "It's time for us to go," he said firmly.

Storm clouds gathered in Rick's blue eyes. "I won't break it, Gray. Honest."

"Maybe some other time," Kathryn put in diplomatically.

With the pragmatism of an eight-year-old, Rick asked, "When can I come back?"

"When you're invited," Gray said quickly.

"When can you invite me?" the boy pressed Kathryn.

Gray tousled the boy's hair. "It's not polite to beg for invitations."

"It's okay," Kathryn responded. "You guys can

come back—'' her gaze met Gray's, her voice lowered ''—anytime.''

A word like ''anytime,'' so simple, so nonspecific, shouldn't have hung in the air like a come-on. Yet it did. And Kathryn Seeger, normally so poised and cool, flushed.

Gray wanted to put her at ease, but all he could manage was a mumbled ''We need to go.''

This time, instead of protesting, she led them to the door. She bent down to give Rick a hug, one the boy returned with more fervor than Gray usually saw him display. Even she looked surprised as Rick released her and went whooping down the steep, outdoor stairway to the back driveway where Gray had parked the Jeep.

''Well...thanks,'' Gray offered, even though his instincts were urging him to escape as quickly as Rick. ''Thanks for feeding Rick.''

She waved off his gratitude. ''It was nothing.''

''Yeah, well...'' He started down the stairs, then turned back to the landing near the door and reached for his wallet. ''I'm sorry. I meant to pay you back for the burgers and beer.''

''It's not necessary.''

''Please.''

''You can get it next time.''

Kathryn bit her lip, realizing that for the second time in less than five minutes she had implied there would be a next time to see Gray Nolan. What she needed was a quick, smooth getaway. ''I think I hear my phone,'' she lied, waving to Gray. ''See you.'' With that, she closed the door. Practically in his face.

But it wasn't until she heard the sound of his Jeep backing out of the driveway that she released a pent-up breath.

What was wrong with her? She didn't want this man in her life. Despite all the good qualities she had glimpsed in him tonight, he had the same overbearing tendencies that had led to the dismissal of other men from her life. Oh, he wasn't a bully or an abuser like the man she had married, but he also wasn't the calm, uncomplicated sort of person Kathryn thought she should be attracted to. She needed to remember the way Gray had come barreling into the store yesterday, barking orders at Ashley and her. She shouldn't focus on the funny flutter in her stomach caused by his admiring glance at her legs. And she most definitely should ignore the maternal ache brought on by Rick's hard little hug.

Most of the time, Kathryn didn't think about wanting children. Her life was full—friends, civic involvement, the shop, a cruise every winter. But just moments ago when that little boy hugged her, she had thought of her own child, the boy who, if she hadn't miscarried, would have been ten next month. Her boy, hers and Darren's, the child whose loss her mother had once referred to as a "blessing in disguise."

Jaw clenched against the regrets that swelled inside her, Kathryn crossed the room and straightened the glass globe on its pedestal. Like Rick, she couldn't resist tracing the outline of the state where they lived. She always loved touching this piece, marveling at the way their entire world was etched into the glass. At Rick's age, she hadn't been allowed to hold the globe, even though her grandmother had given it to her. Kathryn's mother had deemed it far too fragile and valuable to be held. So the globe had sat on a shelf, dusted by the maid, the light inside switched on only occasionally, admired from afar until Kathryn had taken it with her when she left her parents' home for good and moved to Amarillo.

Now, defiantly, Kathryn picked up the globe and gave it a toss. She smiled as she caught it and put it back in place. Then she laughed as she imagined her mother's horror at such irreverent treatment of a valued possession.

Irreverence and defiance.

No doubt, in her mother's mind, those two words were still linked with Kathryn. To Christine Seeger, Kathryn had besmirched the family name. First, by her tempestuous early marriage, then by moving to the West Texas Panhandle, far from the moneyed world of Fort Worth. Christine prided herself on her elegant appearance, her lovely home, her prestigious heart surgeon husband and her brilliant son, Luke, who was a doctor specializing in obstetrics. To her friends, Christine probably passed off Kathryn's defection as an aberration of nature. Or maybe she told them that there'd been a baby switch at the hospital when Kathryn was born.

That idea made Kathryn giggle more. If it wasn't for the fact that she looked so much like Christine, she might believe it herself. Outside of her looks, she wasn't anything like her parents. Her contact with them had dwindled to one strained visit a year, at Thanksgiving. She didn't miss them. As for her brother…Luke was eight years older and had been so intent on school and his burgeoning medical practice that Kathryn felt she barely knew him. Luke had married last year, and she hadn't even attended the wedding. Oh, she had been invited. She had received the same engraved invitation as a couple of hundred other guests. But if Luke had wanted her there, he could have called. She had secretly wanted him to. But even as he didn't reach out to her...she didn't reach out to him.

What a contrast the Seegers presented next to Gray and his brother and sister. All the more reason not to get any romantic notions about Gray. She wasn't qualified to get involved with a real loving family. Or to worry about Rick's emotional struggles. Or fret about Ashley and Jarrett's wedding. As a matter of fact, despite her friendship with the McMullens, it might be a good idea to bow out of this wedding after all. That should effectively put an end to any reason for contact between her and Gray Nolan or either of his siblings.

The only wedding Kathryn needed to think about was the casual garden affair she and Devon were scheduled to cater and coordinate Sunday afternoon. She headed to bed, steadfastly thinking of the flowers that had been ordered to match the bride's buttercup yellow wedding suit.

But she dreamed of a man with blue eyes. That dream man was just about to kiss Kathryn when a pounding on her door woke her up. One bleary glance at the clock revealed it was only six-thirty. What in the world was going on?

Kathryn dragged on her robe as she headed to the door. Swinging it open, she found Ashley and Jarrett on the landing. Ashley was pale, her pretty features scrubbed clean of makeup. Jarrett was flushed, his dark honey hair standing on end as if he had thrust his hands through it a couple of dozen times.

"What in the world are you doing here at this hour?" Kathryn demanded. "You should be home."

Jarrett said, "We know it's early—"

"But I need my dress," Ashley interrupted. "Can I have it?"

"Why?" Kathryn asked, although she was certain she knew the answer.

The two young lovers looked at each other, then Jarrett took Ashley's hand and looked at Kathryn. "We're eloping," he said as if daring her to argue with him. "Right now. Today."

"And even though we're not going to have the big wedding I wanted...I still want my dress." Tears trembled on the tips of Ashley's long, dark lashes. "If I have my dress, at least it will seem more like a wedding."

His dark eyes full of resolve, Jarrett put his arm around Ashley's shoulders. He was tall and lean and strong-looking. Sexy, too, Kathryn realized with a start. Somewhere between now and the last time she had really noticed Jarrett McMullen, he had been transformed from a good-looking boy to an intriguing, masculine presence. Right now, he reminded her of a warrior ready to do battle for his lady.

"We're getting married," he told Kathryn with adult authority. "She'd like her dress. Can we have it?"

Kathryn yearned for the coldheartedness to turn them away. She wished she didn't care about either of them. If that were the case, she might give them the dress and send them off to the justice of the peace. But she couldn't do that. Not to a young man she had known since he was twelve. And not to Gray's sister. Not when Kathryn knew this would break his heart.

So she swung the door open. "Come on in. Let's have a cup of coffee."

"You're not talking us out of this," Ashley said as defiantly as Kathryn remembered saying the same words to her mother.

Kathryn just nodded, closed the door behind them

and rolled up the sleeves of her robe. So much for keeping out of this particular wedding and Gray Nolan's life.

After nearly seven years of being his brother and sister's guardian, after illnesses and arguments and agonizing decisions, Gray knew he should be used to worry. But as the hour approached nine on Saturday morning and he turned his Jeep onto the road leading home, apprehension ate at his gut like battery acid. He hoped Ashley would be waiting for him. As angry as he was about her staying out all night, he really just wanted to know she was safe. He had been on a call at a local ranch since early morning. Despite the turmoil at home, he had work that couldn't be neglected, and in Ashley's absence, he had taken Rick on the call with him.

Gray directed a fond glance at the youngster who had fallen asleep in the passenger seat. Rick hadn't minded coming along. The boy was as crazy about animals as Gray had been as a kid. Maybe Rick would be a vet, as well. They could work together. The pleasant possibility made Gray smile.

That faded, however, as their ranch house came into view. A dark blue car was parked in the driveway, and two women were crossing the front lawn to the porch. *Ashley and Kathryn.* Gravel spewed as Gray turned up the driveway.

He swung out of the Jeep as soon as he cut the engine. He wished Ashley were Rick's age, so he could swat her behind. He wished he could do something to vent his gut-wrenching fear that she was going to mess up her life. He settled for gripping her shoulders and demanding to know if she was all right.

When she assured him she was, he muttered, "Don't pull this again. Please. I've been worried sick. So is Jarrett's dad. I called him about three this morning. He didn't even know Jarrett was in town. The boy was supposed to be in Lubbock, studying for finals."

Head bent, Ashley nodded.

Kathryn said, "I made Jarrett call his father—"

Gray frowned at Kathryn. "How come you made Jarrett call? Were they with you all this time?"

Darting a look at Ashley, Kathryn said, "That's not exactly—"

"Tell him the truth," Ashley said, at last raising her head to look him in the eye. "Jarrett and I spent the night together. We were eloping until Kathryn talked us out of it."

"Eloping?" Gray repeated, the relief over his sister's return rapidly being replaced by anger. "What in the hell—"

"They didn't elope," Kathryn cut in. "I think that's the important thing to remember."

Gray barely heard her. His full attention was on Ashley. "What is wrong with you? First you leave Rick with strangers—"

"And he was fine!" Ashley said, eyes flashing.

"Then you stay out all night," Gray continued, growing hotter by the moment. "Besides the obvious stupidity of getting married at all, how could you think about eloping now? You don't even have your diploma. According to Jarrett's dad, he could blow a whole semester of work if he doesn't pass his finals. What kind of way would that be to start a marriage?" He raked fingers through his hair, feeling as though he was at the end of his rope. "I swear to God, Ashe, I don't know what's wrong with you or Jarrett."

"We're sick of you," she shot back at him. "The way you went off on us last night at the bar was crazy."

"I was concerned about Rick."

"Yeah, you're overly concerned with everything me or Rick do."

"You're my responsibility."

"You're a control freak. And Jarrett and I know you'll do everything you can to stop us from having the wedding we want. We figured eloping was the only way."

"This nonsense has gone far enough."

"Nonsense?" Ashley shouted. "It's not nonsense. We want to be together. We'll be together any way we can."

"If that's so, why isn't Jarrett here with you now, helping you face me? Is he too ashamed? Or just afraid?"

While Ashley struggled to stutter a reply, Kathryn put a calming hand on her arm and faced Gray. "I sent Jarrett back to school. I thought that would be the best, considering all the studying he said he had to do. He wanted to bring Ashley home and talk to you, but I assured him I would take care of her. I figured it might be best to let this episode settle before you and he talked."

"Oh, you did?" Gray made his sarcasm clear. "Thank you so much for your help."

She bristled. "There's no need to be angry with me. I talked them out of eloping, remember?"

Pausing to take a deep breath, Gray reined in his temper before it could stampede again. "I'm sorry," he said to Kathryn, in a tight voice. "Thank you for your help. I feel sure you won't have to deal with this family again.''

"There's still the wedding,'' Ashley snapped. "She's doing the wedding.''

With that, brother and sister were off to the races again. As far as Kathryn was concerned, they were covering the same territory as yesterday, the day before and probably the day before that. And, having done her good deed for the year, she was getting out of here. Without bothering to attempt a goodbye, she started toward her dark blue Acura Legend. She might have made it, too, if Rick hadn't been sitting on the front bumper of Gray's Jeep, staring at his brother and sister with miserable eyes. Two beagles sat on either side of him, looking equally sad.

Shoving her hands deep in the pockets of her crisp white cotton slacks, Kathryn greeted the boy, then nodded toward his dueling siblings. "Their arguments are starting to get on my nerves. How about yours?''

"I wish Gray'd just let her leave. If she'd rather be with Jarrett than me and Gray, then she should go and get it over with.''

The betrayed look on his face plucked at Kathryn's heart. She couldn't do anything his fear that his sister was going to disappear from his life, but she could get him away from the nasty scene before him.

"You hungry?'' she asked. Rick nodded, and she gestured toward the house. "If you'll show me the kitchen, we'll rustle up some breakfast.''

Rick agreed without hesitation. Unnoticed by Gray and Ashley, they walked around back, where a key was hidden under a loose plank in the steps. Then Kathryn followed Rick across the back porch and utility area. With a plaintively meowing cat and the two dogs trailing them, they went into the darkest, most unattractive kitchen she had seen in years.

Done in the avocado greens and oranges made popular by interior decorators decades ago, the room was at odds with the freshly painted and attractive white exterior of the long, rambling house. The room's proportions were wonderful. What could have been an inviting space was terribly unappealing.

"What's the matter?" Rick demanded when she continued to hesitate just inside the kitchen doorway. "Does something smell bad?"

Only then did she realize she had wrinkled her nose in distaste. She shook her head and smiled. "Nothing's wrong. Let's see what's in the refrigerator for breakfast."

Some twenty-five minutes later, Kathryn was scooping scrambled eggs from a skillet to a platter already loaded with browned sausage links. Rick had told her they always had a big breakfast on Saturdays, so she had obliged, even though it had been a long time since she'd had anything more than fruit and cereal before 10:00 a.m. Rick, who chattered the whole time she was cooking, poured juice into the four glasses he had set on the corner table, along with plates, silverware and napkins. Kathryn thought setting four places was optimistic, considering Ashley and Gray remained outside.

As if on cue, a slamming door sounded somewhere in the direction of the front of the house.

"That's Ashley," Rick said with a sigh.

"How do you know?"

"She slams doors that way."

From the back porch came another bang. Not quite as loud. But equally effective.

Rick rolled his eyes. "And that's Gray."

Sure enough, the boy's older brother came stalking into the kitchen. His hands were clenched. His shoulders, beneath his wrinkled denim shirt, were bunched. All in all, he looked like a man ready to go a couple of rounds with a contender.

Kathryn, who was removing a tray of biscuits from the oven, watched him pace around the room before she cleared her throat. He glared at her. She pointed to the coffeemaker.

"I think you could use a cup of that."

"What are you still doing here?"

The rude bellow made Kathryn's eyes narrow. Rick paused, still holding the juice bottle, and stared open-mouthed at his brother.

She forced herself to smile and use her most pleasant tone. "I would have gone, but Rick was hungry. I decided he ought to be fed, considering the other two people in this household were otherwise preoccupied. Do you have a problem with that?" Using only her eyes, she motioned toward the boy. "You don't have a problem, do you?"

Gray looked at his wide-eyed brother. Muscles moved in his throat. His hands unclenched and his shoulders unbunched. "I'm sorry," he said to Kathryn. "I'm not normally so rude."

"Seems I've heard that before," she murmured, still talking as sweetly as she could.

"I'm sorry is all I ever seem to say to you." Gray's tone was nearly as saccharine as hers. "That and thank-you."

"Breakfast's all ready," Rick put in, recovering from his shock over Gray yelling at someone other than a family member. "Kathryn made all your favorites."

"So I see." Gray took the plate of biscuits Kathryn offered. "I guess I owe you some more thanks."

Chair legs scraped across the green linoleum as Rick pulled a chair from the table. "You sit here, Kathryn. Between me and Gray." He darted a look at his brother. "Do you think Ashley wants to eat?"

"Maybe later." With a smile that was on the grim side, Gray set the biscuits on the table and poured himself and Kathryn some coffee.

Kathryn expected to eat in bleak silence. Rick, however, had other ideas. He kept up a running dialogue. About his pets. About school. About where they used to live in Oklahoma. He drew Kathryn out, asking her questions about where she lived when she was his age and about the traveling grandmother she had told him about the night before. Kathryn found it hard to believe this was a child who was often reticent with people he didn't know well. With her, he had been completely open from the very first.

Gray couldn't remain somber or quiet for long around this youngster. Rick soon had his brother telling Kathryn about a fish they had hooked on a deep-sea fishing expedition early last summer. The fish kept getting larger and larger in Gray's tale, the difficulty in landing it more and more extreme, even dangerous. Though she feared she was just being fed a run-of-the-mill fish story, Kathryn actually began to believe Gray. Elbows on the table, she hung on to every word. Finally, she asked where they had mounted this magnificent stuffed trophy.

"Oh, we didn't catch it," Gray said, his expression all innocence. "We decided we couldn't take such an awesome specimen from his natural habitat."

"So it got away," Kathryn accused.

Earnestly, Gray shook his head. "We allowed it to escape, Kathryn. That's not the same thing."

Rick agreed. "There's a big, big difference between letting one go and just losing it." The corners of his mouth trembled as he struggled not to laugh.

"Yeah, sure." Kathryn snorted in disgust. "You guys are the worst. I didn't believe you for a minute."

"You did, too," Rick retorted. "Just like Ashley did. When Gray told her that story, she was crying. She thought the fish almost pulled me overboard. Man, you should have seen her face." His sister's gullibility, for reasons known only to eight-year-olds, was hilarious. Rick laughed so long and so hard that Gray finally had to send him to work off his excess energy in the backyard with his beagles.

Once he was gone, Kathryn sank back in her chair with a sigh.

Gray chuckled. "I know how you feel—like somebody just drained the power in the room."

"He keeps you on your toes, all right."

"I told you that last night."

Standing, Kathryn glanced at the clock. She had called Devon and asked her to watch the shop until noon, and it was time to clear the dishes and be on her way.

Gray stopped her. "I'll take care of this. You've done enough around here for one morning."

Kathryn didn't argue. Dirty dishes were never at the top of her list. "I'd better go."

"I meant what I said," Gray added, getting to his feet. "I'm grateful to you."

"It was just breakfast."

"I'm referring to your talking Ashley out of eloping and then bringing her home."

"It wasn't that hard to talk them out of eloping."

"If that's so, I wish you'd talk her into giving Jarrett back his ring."

"Even my powers of persuasion aren't that strong. The wedding's not off. Not by a long shot." What she didn't tell Gray was that she had dangled the wedding out in front of Ashley like a carrot. All it took was a few reminders of the ceremony, the dress and the reception to convince Ashley to forget this quickie wedding-on-the-run. Gray didn't need to know any of this, however. He'd just get upset again.

"Whatever you said," Gray continued, "it worked. I wish I knew your secret."

"Well, for one thing, I didn't yell." The tart words, clear criticism of his own handling of the matter, slipped out before Kathryn could stop them.

Gray's brow lowered.

Kathryn held up a hand to stave off the onslaught. "Don't say it, Gray. Despite the fact that I keep getting dragged into this, despite the fact that you've asked for my advice several times, I know this is really none of my business and my remark was out of line."

"I think we've all worked pretty hard at making this your business. I'm sorry for that. I just wish you could see things from my perspective."

After being dragged from her bed to convince his sister not to get married, his last comment made Kathryn angry. "If I didn't give a damn for your feelings in this matter, those kids would be on their way to a wedding right now."

"And I appreciate that," Gray repeated. "What I don't think you understand is the responsibility I have to her. Maybe I am overprotective. Maybe I am penning her in. But since she was not quite twelve years old, Ashley has been my responsibility. I'm more her parent than her brother. I can't stand by while she ruins her life. That's what I don't think you get.''

"Oh, I get it." Kathryn struggled hard with her temper. She wanted to leave without a full-scale clash with Gray, but she wanted to make a point with him for Ashley's sake. "What you don't get is how she feels."

"Oh, she's made that clear."

Kathryn just shook her head. "But do you know that she loves Jarrett? Do you hear her when she tells you that?"

"It's not love. It's lust at best."

"And that's something you can just dismiss as nothing?"

"It'll pass."

"I'm glad you're so sure. When I was eighteen and in love...and in lust, if you will...it didn't feel like nothing." She put a hand on her chest, over her heart. "I was so in love, I ached. Being with Darren was all I wanted. I couldn't see past that. I couldn't even see him, really. All I could do was feel. No one could reason with me. It was my parents' attempts to be reasonable that forced the issue, that..."

Kathryn's voice trailed away. She could see by Gray's expression that he didn't care what she was saying, didn't want to hear anyone's opinions but his own. And honestly, they had covered all of this before, to no avail. Dear God, but he was such a stubborn, shortsighted man. One she shouldn't spare another moment's worry over. His problems weren't hers. She didn't need them. With an impatient, dismissive wave of her hand, she started toward the door.

Gray's quiet voice stopped her. "It's hard for me to imagine your being overcome by lust."

She paused, her hand on the door. One part of her told her to leave. The other was curious to know what he meant. Curiosity, always her downfall, won. She turned around. "What does that mean?"

Gray walked toward her, moving with that lazy stride she had admired when he came into the shop yesterday afternoon. "You don't seem the hot-blooded, impetuous type." He came to a stop a few inches from her.

She lifted an eyebrow, hiding her trepidation. "And just what type am I?"

He answered much too fast. "Cool and rich. In control. Sometimes remote. Never impulsive."

The person Gray described was the person Kathryn had worked hard to become. She wanted control, yes, because if she didn't take it, she feared someone else would. She wouldn't be ruled. Not after escaping both her mother's and Darren's grasps. Not ever again.

"Oh, there are things that don't fit," Gray continued when she didn't answer. "Like how nice you are to Rick, and how you seem to really care about Ashley. And..." His gaze seemed to center on her mouth. He looked away, clearing his throat. "Like I said, it's not easy to see you losing your head or your heart."

That statement hit Kathryn between the eyes. She was reminded—sharply—of something she had once said to her mother, that she couldn't imagine Christine Seeger ever being in love. But Kathryn was nothing like her mother. She had never intended to be anything like Christine. Yet if that's how Gray saw her...

"Kathryn?"

She looked at him, not really seeing him, because her eyes had suddenly flooded with tears.

Gray repeated her name. He seemed at a loss.

"Kathryn, I'm sorry. I didn't mean to upset you. As you were talking, I was just trying to imagine you in the same situation as Ashley, and I couldn't quite..."

Summoning all her hard-won control, Kathryn blinked back the silly tears. *What was wrong with her? She didn't cry like this.* "I need to go."

He touched her arm. "You sure?"

She shook off his detaining hand.

"I said too much, I know—"

"No, you didn't," she insisted, turning once more to go. "I'll..." She stopped when she realized she'd been about to say she would see him. But she didn't want to see him again. She settled on a terse "Good-bye."

But Gray couldn't let her go. Not when she looked this crestfallen. He caught her arm again. "I'm sorry, Kathryn. We don't know each other well, and I should have kept my mouth shut—"

"Don't worry about it," she said calmly.

"Damnation," he muttered. "Why is it that all I seem to do is apologize to you?"

She said nothing, and he felt foolish. Like the class geek who had just insulted the prom queen. He didn't know what to do with his hands. But because it felt as if he should be doing something with them, he placed them on Kathryn's shoulders. She seemed surprised, but didn't move. She stared up at him, her green eyes full of an emotion so closely shuttered that he could only guess what it might be. It was only when he kissed her that he had a hint....

Yes, he kissed her. It happened before he thought, before he had time to tell himself someone as cool and polished and in control as Kathryn Seeger wouldn't be interested in kissing him. But her lips beneath his weren't cool at all. They were warm and responsive. She tasted of orange juice, and she made him feel as hot as the West Texas sunshine spilling through the windows of his ugly kitchen. With this kiss, she disputed everything he had said about her controlled, chilly manner.

Just when he thought the kiss might end, Kathryn lifted her hands to his chest, spread her fingers wide against his denim shirt and tilted her head to the side. The kiss deepened instantly. He wondered if she could feel his heart, beating hard enough to burst through the skin. He hoped she could feel how sweet he thought she was, and how perfect this moment was for him.

She drew away. He brought her back to him for another kiss.

Then another.

Another.

Each bolder, longer, harder.

Gray figured they might have stood there kissing for a long, long time if Ashley hadn't come into the room. And if his sister had been quiet, if she had backed away and behaved with the tact and respect she was always wanting from him, he thought he and Kathryn might have reached a place where few people went from merely kissing.

As it was, Ashley made a sound, and Kathryn stepped back. Kathryn looked at him and at Ashley. Color flooded her face. And she left. Without a word.

Before Ashley could make a smart-alecky comment, Gray followed Kathryn's trail out the door. He just wasn't up to a critique from his kid sister about his romantic style. At the moment, all he wanted to do was get busy, get so busy he wouldn't have to think about how nice it had felt to hold Kathryn in his arms.

Chapter Four

Kathryn threw open the door to Blue Heaven Weddings' catering kitchen and stalked inside, grumbling under her breath.

Devon looked up from the bowl of icing she was removing from the electric mixer. "What in the world is wrong?"

Her jaw clenched, Kathryn said, "Mrs. Alfred G. Hunsucker."

"Don't tell me she's changing something else about her granddaughter's bridesmaids' luncheon."

Kathryn waved two pink roses in the air. "She just dropped these by. She says to make sure the icing on the cake is tinted this exact shade. Can you imagine that? It's closing time, the luncheon is tomorrow, and that empty-headed woman comes traipsing by with these. What if the cakes were already decorated?"

"Then we'd scrape the icing off." Laughing, Devon

reached for the roses and compared them to the confection in the bowl. "I was afraid she was switching menus for the eighth time in two weeks. I can tint icing, but I'm not sure what we'd do with the ten pounds of mandarin-orange chicken salad I just put in the refrigerator."

Kathryn paced about the sun-splashed, ultramodern kitchen she had remodeled last year after hiring Devon and deciding to increase the catering business. "Mrs. Hunsucker annoys me to death," she muttered.

"She's no worse than most people we deal with. They want what they're paying for." Devon sent Kathryn a long, considering look as she added a drop of red food coloring to the icing. "I think there's something else bothering you."

Coming to a stop beside the other woman, Kathryn forced herself to take a calming breath. "I'm tired. It's only Tuesday afternoon, but it's already been a long week."

"And is being tired the reason you jump every time the phone rings or someone comes through the door?"

Pointedly ignoring her friend's inquisitive gaze, Kathryn nodded. "If we weren't heading into our busiest season, I might take a vacation."

"You'd get out of Dodge, so to speak."

Kathryn frowned at her. "What does that mean?"

"Just that you've been as ill as a newly branded calf since you came back from Gray Nolan's place Saturday morning."

"I have not."

"Have so."

"Not!" Kathryn retorted, even as she realized the childish exchange was proving Devon's point.

Grinning, Devon set the icing bowl under the stationary electric mixer for a moment's more of blending. A quick comparison with Mrs. Hunsucker's roses showed the frosting color to be a perfect match.

Kathryn tried to change the subject. "Look at that. You're a genius in the kitchen. Mrs. Hunsucker will be so pleased."

Devon was not easily swayed from the subject of Gray Nolan. "You might as well just tell me about Gray," she said, switching off the mixer.

Kathryn took a spoon from a nearby drawer, ignored her friend and sampled the icing. The younger woman had been attempting to discuss Gray with Kathryn ever since Saturday. So far, Kathryn had gotten away with a few vague comments. She thought that if she didn't talk about that kiss she and Gray had shared, she might eventually be able to pretend it never happened. She was doing everything she could, even avoiding returning a call from Ashley, to keep Gray Nolan as far from her thoughts as possible.

"I know something's up," Devon insisted.

Still ignoring her, Kathryn licked her spoon. "This is terrific. Maybe soon we'll be doing so many luncheons, parties and receptions that you can concentrate on this part of the business exclusively. I'll hire another part-time clerk to help me with the shop. Food is where your real talent lies."

"Thanks, boss." Devon took the spoon from Kathryn's hand. "You can talk all around this for as long as you want, but I'm eventually going to get the truth out of you. So why not save us both a lot of time?"

Sighing in defeat, Kathryn slumped against the counter. Quickly, not allowing time for comment, she told Devon the whole story of Saturday's events, ending with a blunt "And then he kissed me."

Devon, who was putting the frosting in a pastry bag, looked up, her eyes wide. "*Really* kissed you?"

"*Really, really.*"

"And how was it?"

Kathryn admitted out loud what she hadn't wanted to admit to herself. "It was wonderful."

Squealing in delight, Devon dropped the pastry bag to the counter. She squeezed Kathryn's arm. "This is great."

Glaring at her, Kathryn said, "No, it's not. I didn't want him to kiss me. I don't want to be interested in him."

"Why not?"

"Because he's opinionated."

"So are you," Devon pointed out with a devilish grin.

Kathryn let that pass. "He's overbearing."

"He was perfectly charming when he came by Friday afternoon to apologize."

That was true, but Kathryn didn't want to think about any of Gray's good qualities. "Besides all of that, he has a terribly complicated life."

"Who doesn't?"

"Oh, stop being so reasonable," Kathryn snapped. "Gray Nolan is simply not my kind of man."

Returning to her pastry bag, Devon said dryly, "If we waited for who we envision as our Prince Charmings, we'd be alone the rest of our lives."

"I don't mind being alone."

"Hah!"

"I don't," Kathryn insisted. "My life is very full." Devon didn't know about Kathryn's ex-husband, and she probably couldn't understand that any loneliness

Kahtryn might feel was preferable to being under the control of a man.

Devon screwed a decorative tip on the bag. "So you're not curious?"

"About what?"

"What it might be like to kiss him again?"

Kathryn let out a breath. "There's a lot more than kisses to consider." A lot more. The last time she'd let emotions rule, she wound up in a disastrous, abusive marriage.

Her pastry bag poised over one of two sheet cakes she needed to decorate, Devon gave her a skeptical glance.

Kathryn decided to admit to a secret wish. "Maybe I wouldn't mind getting to know him a little better."

"What's stopping you?"

"He hasn't called." And Kathryn should be relieved, but she couldn't deny a spark of disappointment. God, what was wrong with her?

"Call him," Devon suggested.

"I couldn't do that."

"This isn't high school," Devon said. "You are twenty-nine years old, a successful businesswoman and someone the man's obviously attracted to. You can call him. No one will tell your mommy," she teased.

"I wouldn't know what to say."

Another grin flitted across Devon's face. "Just say what comes naturally. Something like, 'I want your body. When can we meet?'"

"Don't be ridiculous," Kathryn said.

"So you don't want his body?"

Color flamed in Kathryn's cheeks. "That's not the point."

Devon laughed. "It's so nice to see you admitting to a few human emotions."

"What does that mean?"

The younger woman turned back to her cakes, shrugging. "You're just so perfect, Kathryn."

"You, of all people, know I'm not perfect at all."

"But you always give the illusion of perfection. That's how I knew something was up these past few days. You've been distracted and short-tempered. Usually you're so calm and controlled."

Her words were entirely too similar to those Gray had used to describe Kathryn on Saturday. That meant her worst fears were true, Kathryn admitted bleakly to herself. She was becoming her mother. And that was the last thing she had ever wanted.

Glancing up from the pink rose she had swirled onto the cake, Devon said, "Gee, Kathryn, there's no reason to look so depressed. Being perfect isn't a crime."

"It can be."

"What do you mean?"

"Perfection is a cold state of affairs, Devon."

"But you're not a cold person."

"Not yet anyway."

Devon frowned. "What's that supposed to mean?"

Not answering, Kathryn gave her a distracted pat on the arm. "Thanks."

"For what?"

"I'll let you know."

Feeling her friend's puzzled gaze following her, Kathryn went out to lock up the shop for the day. She took care of some bookkeeping, returned to the kitchen to assist Devon with a few details for tomorrow's luncheon, then retired for the evening to her apartment.

No matter where she went, a telephone was always at the corner of her field of vision.

Devon's command sounded clear in her head. *Call him.*

Did she dare?

Daring would place her heart in jeopardy. Though Gray was still a relative stranger, he represented the risk she had avoided since her marriage ended.

Gray's description of her also echoed like thunder in her brain. *Cool and rich. In control. Sometimes remote. Never impulsive.*

Damn it, she didn't want to be remote or controlled. As a girl, she had been headstrong and daring, always ready for adventure. Her mother had despaired of her propensity to disappear for hours into the woods near their suburban home and return with torn clothes and skinned knees. As a teenager, she had been a risk taker, a leader, always up for fun. When had that part of her disappeared? Had her failed marriage taken that from her for good? She didn't want to think that Darren had exercised that final bit of control over her. But if he had changed her so profoundly...

That question tugged at Kathryn for most of the evening. The person she had once been would follow Devon's advice and call Gray. She hadn't felt cold and controlled in his arms. She had felt wild, hot, impetuous. Maybe she should flirt with him, invite him over for dinner, kiss him again, seduce him...

The very thought sent Kathryn into a state of high anxiety. She put on her oldest, sloppiest pajamas, the least sexy and most imperfect garment she owned. She was striving to look and behave less like her mother, less perfect. But she knew the one way to assure herself she wasn't slipping into total Christine Seeger-like perfection was to call Gray.

By the time the clock's hands slipped past nine-thirty, Kathryn knew she was either going to call Gray or risk a heart attack. She made herself as comfortable as possible in the corner of the sofa and picked up the phone.

He answered on the second ring.

She opened her mouth, but no sound escaped.

"Hello?" he repeated, an edge of irritation to his voice.

Her vocal cords unfroze. "Gray, this is Kathryn."

"Oh...uh...hello." He paused, cleared his throat. "How are you?"

"I'm okay. I hope I'm not calling too late."

"Of course not. I just finished wrestling Rick into bed."

"Wrestling?"

"Bedtime's always a struggle on school nights."

"He's okay, isn't he?"

"He's fine."

Kathryn's face flushed. She was feeling more and more foolish by the minute. "How's Ashley?"

Gray sighed.

"I take that to mean nothing's changed."

"The wedding's still on, I'm afraid. Hasn't she talked to you?"

"She did call...."

"Oh." Again, he paused. "I guess you were calling to talk to her, then."

"No," she said quickly. Too quickly. The heat in her face streaked down her neck. "What I meant was that I...I'm calling you."

He said nothing. For a long, long, awkward time, only silence emanated from his end of the line.

Kathryn closed her eyes, cursing the impulse that had led her to this horrible moment of rejection.

She heard Gray let out a breath. Then he murmured, "I've been thinking about you."

Her eyes flew open. *Oh, God, maybe abject mortification wasn't at hand.* "You have?"

"A lot."

She risked a soft "I've been thinking about you, too."

He cleared his throat again. "The way you left Saturday—"

"Oh, Gray." Sinking lower in her sofa, Kathryn pressed her burning cheek to the cushioned armrest. "I can't believe I ran out like that."

"I can't believe Ashley just stood there, gaping at us like she did. For a mature, engaged woman, as she calls herself these days, she was very rude. I'm sorry."

"But I shouldn't have run out. That was silly. I acted like I've never been..." She swallowed. The heat from her neck was rapidly making its way down the rest of her body.

"Never been kissed?" Gray supplied, his voice deepening, taking on a near-teasing quality. "Something tells me you've had a little experience in that department."

"You, too."

His sigh reached right through the phone line and stroked its way down the same path as her blush. She wondered what Gray would say if he knew just hearing his voice and thinking of their kiss caused her to flush scarlet from head to toe. But imagining his reaction only intensified the heat. A pleasant ache began in the most intimate parts of her body.

"Kathryn?" Gray murmured.

"Yeah?"

"I wasn't sure how you felt about me kissing you."

Thinking of the way she had clung to him, Kathryn had to chuckle. "You mean I didn't make it obvious?"

"Well..." He laughed. "When it was happening, I was pretty sure you were enjoying yourself."

"Only pretty sure?"

"Make that very sure."

"And how about you?"

He paused. His voice roughened even further. "I'm not certain I should tell you exactly how I reacted."

"Why's that?"

"This isn't one of those 1-900 sex lines."

So their kiss had aroused him. Kathryn bit her lip, trying to set aside the erotic pictures that were flashing through her brain. Images of Gray's muscular body, taut and hard and...

"Kathryn?" Gray asked when the silence stretched between them. "I'm sorry. I didn't mean to offend you."

"I'm not offended," she assured him, her voice shaky.

"You sure?"

"No, I'm..." She caught herself before she could say something embarrassing. Then she remembered she didn't want to be cautious, or cool. So she took the plunge. "If you want to know the truth," she whispered, burrowing deeper into the cushions of her sofa, as if the furniture could protect her from herself, "instead of offended, I'm kind of...uh...turned on."

The sound he made was somewhere between a groan and a sigh.

The silence that followed that sound made her want to die. "Now I've offended you."

"That's not what I'd call what I'm feeling."

So he was as hot and bothered as she was. Kathryn squeezed her legs together, enjoying the ripple of pleasure that resulted. "I can't believe we're having this conversation," she said.

"Me, neither," he admitted gruffly. "But it sure beats the hell out of the cop show that's on TV."

"The one that always posts a parent's advisory at the beginning?"

"That's the one."

From her nest in her sofa cushions, Kathryn reached for the television remote control on the coffee table. She switched on the set and flipped channels until she located the program Gray was talking about. "Is this show a particular favorite of yours?"

"I never miss it."

She glanced at the screen. She knew enough about the program to recognize the romantic lead, who appeared headed to bed with someone. "It looks as if the show's heating up. Maybe I should let you go."

"Don't," Gray protested quickly. "I can watch TV anytime."

"You could call me back." On the television, the camera was panning over two sleek, naked bodies. They moved together, then apart in a mesmerizingly fluid rhythm, the lights and shadows showing just enough to be provocative. If Kathryn hadn't already been aroused, she had a feeling this program would have done the trick.

"Are you watching this?" Gray whispered.

"Yeah."

"Pretty hot stuff for network television."

She hoped her breathing didn't sound as loud and irregular as it felt. "It's tastefully done," she offered in a voice that let her down by squeaking.

"I guess so," Gray agreed. He made a choked sound just as the woman on the screen straddled her partner's lean hips.

Kathryn, whose body had become one pulsating ache, was jealous of the sighs of completion shared by the television couple just before the screen faded to black and the credits began to roll. It was several moments before she realized Gray was saying something to her.

"What?"

His voice was ragged sounding. "I said I'd like to see you again."

"When?"

He chuckled. "Would right now be too soon?"

She laughed, as well. "I'm afraid you think I'm a terribly forward woman. Kissing you Saturday, calling you, talking like this."

"I kissed you, remember?"

"But—"

"And I haven't done anything to discourage the direction our conversation has taken."

"But I should..." She swallowed the words. She had been about to say she should have been in control, but impulse had been what she sought when she made the call. She needed to focus on being impulsive. Unfortunately, however, caution was edging its way into her mind. She said, "Gray, I'm feeling foolish."

"Why?"

"Because all I was thinking when I called you was that maybe we could have dinner again sometime."

"You feel like our conversation skipped a couple of steps?"

"Maybe."

"Then we'll backtrack when I see you tomorrow." She gripped the receiver. "Tomorrow?"

"How about six-thirty? I could pick you up at the shop. We'll go get something to eat, talk…" His pause was a fill-in-the-blank tantalization.

"Make it seven," Kathryn said, trying hard not to sound anxious. "I have a busy day tomorrow."

"Then I'll see you."

Kathryn hung up the phone and hugged herself, feeling totally, completely and absolutely…*perfect.* And yet not one bit like her mother. The sensation was exhilarating.

Gray flipped off his cordless phone and tossed it into the tangled covers of his bed. God, he hurt. His muscles were stretched as tight as fence wire. And he was harder than Texas mud baked under an August sun. What was wrong with him, sighing and moaning over the phone to Kathryn as if she were a pay-by-the-minute sex operator? But he hadn't been able to stop imagining what she might look like, lying in her own bed in a satin teddy, whispering to him, her skin fragrant and soft. He pictured Kathryn sliding her body over his in much the same way the television actress had slipped onto her partner.…

With a groan, he turned off that image. If he kept this up, he was going to explode. As it was, each movement was torture. His sex strained against the front of his boxers.

Cursing his weakness, he stood, stripped off his boxers and headed for a cold shower. The water cooled his ardor, but the momentary release couldn't erase the thoughts of Kathryn that had been nagging at him for the past few days.

Maybe it was lingering sexual frustration that caused Gray to frown the next evening when he slowed his Jeep to a stop in front of Kathryn's shop. He had been distracted all day. But he had things other than frustration to frown about, as well. Ashley was still barely speaking to him, and Rick was in a hyper mood, making Gray feel guilty about leaving him in his sister's care for the evening. Perhaps he should call this dinner with Kathryn off, maybe he should go home...

The thought had no more entered his mind than Kathryn appeared in the shop's doorway. She stepped out onto the porch of the renovated older home and looked at him. In a short, pleated pink skirt and matching sleeveless blouse, she looked trim and pretty, fresh as a newly cut rose. Even from this distance, Gray reacted to the sight of her. All worry about Ashley and Rick fled as he got out of the Jeep and crossed the parking lot to Kathryn's side.

Her green eyes were wide with concern. "Is there something wrong?"

Only that you make me as hot as a fifteen-year-old with a centerfold. Gray ignored that thought and shook his head.

"You were sitting out here for so long, I was afraid there was a problem."

"Were you watching for me?"

Her pale, delicate skin flushed nearly as pink as her blouse as she led the way inside. "I was closing up for the day and couldn't help but notice your Jeep out-side.''

"I was afraid I was too early," Gray said, watching greedily as her slender, rosy-tipped fingers turned the key in the front-door lock and pulled down the shade on the window. *He wondered how those fingers would feel against his skin.*

"You're right on time." She faced him, looking un-certain of herself, biting her bottom lip.

He wanted her moist, red mouth beneath his again. Soon.

Gray's hands fisted at his sides as he told himself to hang on. He forced himself to look away from her. "Is everyone gone for the day?"

"Devon and my other part-time employee left a while ago. They did a luncheon today, a big one, and I sent them home early..." As if she realized she was chattering, Kathryn stopped.

"I hope you're hungry," Gray said, still looking anywhere but at her. There was a pause. He glanced at her, surprised by the turmoil he glimpsed on her face. He took a step forward. "Kathryn?"

"Let's go." Her hand appeared to shake as she flipped off the light switch beside the door. Though it was still light outside, the shop's showroom was plunged into gloom. Gray found himself holding his breath. "We'll go out the back door," Kathryn mur-mured. "So I can set the burglar alarm."

Gray nodded, but didn't move.

For a moment, neither did she. Then she started for-ward, brushing past him. Her fragrance—light, femi-nine, memorable—moved over him like a caress. He touched her arm. She froze. He turned her to face him.

"We should go," she said.

Though he nodded, he still didn't move toward the rear of the store. Instead, he reached up and traced one finger down the curve of her cheek. "Just as I imagined," he murmured.

"What?"

"Your skin. So soft." He cupped her face in his hand. "I've been going crazy, thinking about you. Ever since last night."

She closed her eyes and covered the hand he held to her cheek with her own. "Last night on the phone was wild. I'm not usually like that."

"Neither am I."

"But I don't want you to think..." Muscles moved in her throat as she swallowed. Her hand fell to her side, then lifted in a helpless gesture. She looked at him in mute appeal.

He thought he knew what she was trying to say. "You don't want me to think you're some loose woman. I don't. Nothing you said last night made me think anything that hadn't occurred to me before. In fact, I've been pretty much a lost cause since Saturday."

Her eyes gleamed in the gathering twilight. "Saturday you said I was cold."

"I did?" Touching her, smelling her perfume and yearning like the devil to kiss her, Gray was having a hard time concentrating on what she was saying.

"You called me cool and controlled."

"I was wrong."

He fanned his fingers upward, lifting her hair from her cheek. The tendrils slipped like black silk from his touch, swinging down to graze the creamy skin at the side of her neck. Drawn to that spot, he pushed her hair aside and leaned forward to kiss her. The moment his lips touched her, she sucked in her breath. She lifted her chin, arching toward him. Her skin warmed as his mouth opened, as he moved his tongue up her neck, tasting her sweetness.

Her hands lifted and came to rest on his back, fingers opening, then closing into fists. She let out her breath slowly, and he moved his attention from her neck to her mouth. Her lips parted instantly, with no pressure from his own. She accepted his tongue into her mouth with a soft moan of pleasure, a sound that intensified in direct proportion to their kiss.

In only moments, Gray had backed Kathryn against the wall beside the door. He was dimly aware of something soft and light falling on his head. Silk, he thought. He brushed it away, concentrating instead on getting as close to Kathryn as humanly possible. She seemed to have the same purpose in mind. For she didn't protest when he snaked one of his legs between hers. She said nothing when he dragged the hem of her skirt upward, so that his knee could press against the juncture of her thighs. And when his other hand cupped her right breast, her only response was an urgent, whispered "Yes."

Even with that encouragement, Gray hesitated over the buttons of her blouse. Drawing back, her gaze steady on his, she undid them for him, pulling the blouse free of her skirt's waistband. The blouse fell open, revealing breasts that swelled gently above her bra's lacy white cups. He brushed his fingers down her shadowy cleavage. His fingertips skimmed the nipples that strained against their fabric constraint.

Kathryn closed her eyes as Gray bent forward to allow his lips the same exploration as his fingers. His tongue circled her hardening nipples, moistening the lace of her bra, ministering to one, and then the other breast. All the while, his leg pressed between hers. Her hips rotated downward to meet that pressure, and her hands settled on the buckle of his belt.

It was all happening fast. *Too fast,* a voice inside Gray whispered. He tried to ignore the warning, tried to concentrate on the feminine curves beneath his hands and his mouth. He tried thinking only of the hardening ache of his sex, of his frustration, of how good it would feel to slide inside Kathryn's body. It had been so long since he had been with anyone. Completion was so close. He didn't want to stop. Kathryn's fingers unfastened his belt, unzipped his jeans. Through the thin material of his briefs, she cupped him, stroking his length. Against his mouth, she sighed her approval.

And he had to stop.

The knowledge hit him like a pail of cold water. Groaning, he took his mouth from her breasts. He stilled the movements of her hand and let his leg slide from between hers. Though she protested, he brought their frenzied, frantic motions to an end.

He still held her. With infinite care, he wrapped her tightly in his arms, tucking her head just beneath his chin, murmuring soft, soothing words.

When his own pulse had stopped hammering, he pulled away. The darkness in the shop had grown to the point where he couldn't clearly read her expression. But he felt her unease.

"What happened?" she finally asked.

"Remember those steps we skipped last night?" He traced the outline of her mouth with his finger. "I think we just jumped over a couple dozen more."

She turned her head, eyes downcast. "I get this feeling that you and I are hopelessly out of sync."

"Maybe not."

"Well, I'm feeling pretty humiliated right now, so..." She extricated herself from his grasp, turning away as she buttoned and straightened her blouse and skirt.

Gray attended to his own clothing. Minutes passed, and Kathryn continued to stand with her back to him, her arms folded.

Earnestly, he said, "I never intended to embarrass you. That's not why I stopped."

"Well, you stopped for some reason. Probably because you didn't want to go on."

"Did it feel like I didn't want you?"

She shrugged, and he walked around in front of her, determined that she look at him. She shifted her gaze stubbornly away, but he touched her face, gently forcing her to meet his gaze.

"You *felt* how much I wanted you."

"Yes," she answered, briefly closing her eyes before looking at him again. "The same as you felt how much I wanted you."

"I stopped because I didn't think we should do it that way."

"Who made you boss?"

The tart question, so in keeping with the woman he had met only days ago, made Gray laugh. "I guess you're right," he admitted. "I should have stepped back, quietly voiced my concerns and then let you make the final determination."

"Oh, damn." Raking a hand through her hair, Kathryn walked over to the waist-high carved wooden counter that faced the front door. She switched on an antique, fringed lamp before looking at Gray again. "I suppose I should thank you. I might be feeling even more humiliated if we had continued.''

The lamp's soft glow outlined the gentle curves of her body to perfection. Gray knew a moment's regret for his restraint. ''Actually, I think we might have been feeling satisfied.''

Kathryn shook a finger at him. ''You're scary, Gray Nolan. I don't think you know your own mind.''

''You're right,'' he agreed. ''And that's the real reason I put the brakes on. We've barely known each other a week. How could we go through with what we started?''

''I don't know.'' Kathryn crossed to the wall beside the door and rescued several lengths of silk and satin from the floor. She shook her head as she folded the delicate fabrics and placed them on the shelf from which they had been knocked during her passionate frenzy with Gray. ''I don't know what's happened to me. I've never behaved this way with any man.''

''Come on,'' Gray murmured. ''You were married.''

''When Darren and I started dating, I was a seventeen-year-old virgin who still thought my mother would be able to tell what I'd been doing just by looking at me. I held Darren off—without much difficulty—for almost six months.''

''Until you got married?''

Instead of answering, Kathryn settled the last bit of material on the shelf. She walked slowly back to the desk, where she leaned against the corner, her arms once more folded across her midriff. She repeated what she had tried to tell him before things got wild. ''I didn't like what you said to me Saturday, about my being cold.''

"You shouldn't have paid any attention to that. I have very little to base any opinion of you on."

"But I think that's why I've acted this way with you. I've been trying to prove something."

"To me?"

"To myself."

Gray felt a familiar stirring of unease, the same discomfort he had felt at the party on Friday, when that blonde had assumed he was Kathryn's "walk on the wild side."

Kathryn continued, "When you said that you couldn't imagine my being impulsive and passionate like Ashley, I decided to prove you wrong."

His chest tightened. "Is that why you called me?"

She was silent, studying him intently. Then she turned away again and fiddled with the fringe on the lamp. "I wish it were that simple."

"What does that mean?"

"I wish I wasn't quite so attracted to you on so many different levels."

He knew a moment's relief that he hadn't been just a wild and crazy experiment in passion. But because her words were such a direct reflection of his own feelings and concerns, Gray was silent, fumbling for a reply.

"You don't have to say anything." Kathryn's attention was still riveted on the lamp's fringe. "I'm not fishing for you to tell me about your own feelings."

He finally found his voice and surprised himself with his reply. "Do you really have to fish?"

She looked at him then. A steady, intense look.

He went on, trying not to waver under her regard. "If what I was feeling were just superficial, I might have found what I was looking for a few minutes ago, up against that wall."

Her gaze fell, the lamplight highlighting the crimson staining her cheeks. "That sounds pretty cheap."

"Which is exactly why I stopped. Because you're not cheap." He hesitated, then plunged ahead, his voice gruff. "And, on many, many different levels, I am very attracted to you."

Her hands fell from the lamp fringe. She clasped them together in front of her, looking anxious. "You don't sound pleased about being attracted to me," she said finally.

Gray was rapidly regretting his decision not to make love to her tonight, regretting his confession about his feelings. He should have taken what she offered, kept it quick and superficial. He didn't need a multifaceted attraction to this woman, to any woman. He had enough problems.

Finally, because he knew he needed to answer Kathryn, he said, "I wasn't looking for this. For you."

"Same here."

"My track record with women is pretty bad."

"Oh, and I'm such a relationship whiz." She laughed shortly. "I was divorced at nineteen, remember? And for ten years, I've avoided repeating any part of that mistake."

At least she had taken the plunge. Gray couldn't even lay claim to trying. No one could say he was commitment-shy, given that he had dedicated most of his life to his half siblings, but neither had he given himself completely to a woman. At least that was what Gina had said just before she broke their engagement. He had always dismissed her accusations as an excuse to avoid the messy entanglements of his life. But Ashley had said many of the same things to him recently, when she questioned his single status and said he had turned old and bitter before his time.

Gray didn't want to believe that either Gina or Ashley was right. But now...now, as he stood watching beautiful, exciting Kathryn Seeger, as he felt a familiar stirring of apprehension, he wondered if his sister and ex-fiancée were more insightful than he had given them credit for.

Kathryn lifted her chin, every inch the poised, cool and collected woman she had appeared from the moment Gray met her. Only now he'd had a glimpse of the fire that lay just beneath the serene surface. He wondered if he could live with the regret if he never explored the depths of her passion.

"What do you think we should do about us?" Kathryn asked, drawing him from his reverie.

Frowning, he tucked a hand in his jeans pocket and rocked forward on the balls of his feet. "Damned if I know."

She laughed, softly at first and then louder. "At least you're honest."

"Well?" he demanded. "What do you want to do?"

She bit her lip. "Have dinner, maybe?"

He blinked. "What?"

Kathryn took several slow, measured steps toward him, explaining, "The way I see it, we have two choices. We could each turn tail and run."

"That's appealing."

"Or we could get to know one another."

Gray was a man who didn't like admitting to fear. But this slim woman, with her shining hair and bright eyes, scared the hell out of him. Those stirrings of unease he had felt only a moment ago were now a hard ball of alarm. That ball had settled in his gut and should have been enough to send him off into the night, never to return. Shockingly, however, he didn't want to run.

What he wanted was to have dinner with Kathryn.

Laugh with her.

Talk to her.

Kiss her good-night on her doorstep.

And do the same thing all over again tomorrow.

What he needed to do was not take this so seriously. In a life filled with responsibilities, he had rarely just gone with the flow. Maybe he should. Ashley had been telling him for quite a while that he needed some fun in his life. Perhaps getting to know Kathryn Seeger— getting to know her very well—was just the medicine he needed.

After all, Kathryn had admitted to the same sorts of fears he had. She had told him she wasn't looking for marriage or the sort of long-term commitment that Gray felt was an impossible goal for him. So, despite the many levels on which he found her appealing, surely they could keep things steady and light and un-complicated. God, that would be nice, to have at least one part of his life turn out to be simple.

This could be good. Dating Kathryn. Having fun with her. Very soon making love to her in the slow, complete way she deserved....

"Gray?" she said, looking to him for an answer. "What do you want to do?"

He put out his hand. "Is Chinese okay for dinner?"

Kathryn hesitated for half a beat, her gaze giving him another slow, steady scan. Then she slipped her fingers into his and smiled. "Perfect." The smile died, replaced by concern. "I mean perfect in the best pos-sible sense, of course."

Gray had no idea why the word "perfect" would be cause for alarm, but he laughed with her as they headed to the back door of the shop.

Chapter Five

With one hand, Kathryn held up a baby blue, off-the-shoulder bridesmaid gown. With the other, she displayed a fuchsia, full-skirted dress. "I like this color," she said to Ashley, nodding at the more vibrant dress. "But this style." She indicated the first gown. "What about you?"

Stepping back, Ashley cocked her head to the side. "Actually. . ." Her tawny eyes skipped from one dress to the other, avoiding Kathryn's gaze as she had been doing since arriving at the shop. "Actually...I hate them both."

Behind them, Devon groaned. Frowning, Ashley looked at her and then away, her lips tightening in displeasure.

"Don't mind me," Devon murmured. "I'll be out in the kitchen, baking a cake." With a disgusted glance at Ashley's back, she lifted the numerous bridesmaid dresses that Ashley had already turned down from the dressing-room rack.

When Devon was gone, Ashley looked at Kathryn. At least in her direction. Her voice was anything but sincere. "I'm sorry if I'm being difficult, but I'll know what I want when I see it."

Very carefully, Kathryn hung up the dresses she held. Ever since Ashley had found Kathryn and Gray kissing nearly three weeks ago, the younger woman had grown increasingly remote. Ashley and Gray were still operating under an armed truce regarding the wedding, but Kathryn didn't see why she was getting the cold shoulder, as well. Kathryn and Gray were seeing each other every day, and that meant there was frequent interaction with Ashley and Rick.

The young boy was warm and accepting. He loved telling Kathryn knock-knock jokes, probably because she laughed at even the corniest punch line. Surprisingly, he liked being hugged, too, accepting her frequent embraces without the squirming protests she expected of a boy his age. And something about her sense of order appealed to him, as well. When Kathryn helped prepare dinner at Gray's, Rick set the table just right, the way she preferred, and he submitted to her inspections of his freshly scrubbed hands without too much trouble. Oh, he groused and called her a fuddy-duddy, but Kathryn didn't miss his pleased little smile when she praised him. Or when she read him a book. Or when he cuddled between her and Gray when they watched a movie on television. Rick had become a third wheel in their romance. Gray had grumbled about it just last night, but Kathryn didn't mind too much. This active little boy was working his way into her heart.

On the other hand, Ashley regarded Kathryn with what appeared to be growing suspicion. She had been positively sullen earlier this week when Kathryn came to her graduation, and she had missed two appointments to look at bridesmaid dresses. Until now, Kathryn had been trying to ignore Ashley's attitude, but it was time to clear the air.

"Is there a problem?" she said to Ashley, who was fingering the blue gown with open distaste.

"I just don't like the dresses."

"I'm talking about a problem between us."

Ashley brushed a strand of blond hair back from her cheek. "I don't know what you mean."

"You act like you're angry with me."

The younger woman was silent.

"Is it because of Gray and me?"

Ashley's features tightened, but she remained silent.

"I know we probably embarrassed you," Kathryn murmured. "When you walked in on us in your kitchen, kissing…"

"That was no big deal," Ashley snapped.

Perplexed, Kathryn studied her angry profile. "Then what's wrong?"

Her voice low and hostile, Ashley said, "I know he's working on you."

"What does that mean?"

The younger woman faced Kathryn. "I know Gray's converting you over to his side."

"His side?"

"About the wedding," Ashley retorted impatiently. "Hasn't he about convinced you to talk me out of it?"

Frowning, Kathryn gestured toward the dresses she had just shown Ashley. "Does this look like I'm trying to talk you out of something?"

"You're just going along for now. Sort of like Jarrett's father."

"Jarrett's father likes you a lot."

"But he still has hopes we'll call off the wedding. He's just more subtle about it than Gray."

Kathryn felt she couldn't divulge what she knew about Rex McMullen's thinking, although the man's reverse psychology had clearly not fooled Ashley.

"What about you?" Ashley asked.

The blunt question made Kathryn blink.

"I'd like to hear your opinion about the wedding."

Again, Kathryn gestured to the gowns. "Goodness, isn't it clear—"

"No," the young woman interrupted. "I'm not clear on it, and I'd really like to know what you think." Her brashness disappeared quickly as she bent her head and scuffed her worn loafer along the carpeted floor. "I thought you were on our side."

Her forlorn tone touched Kathryn, who moved forward and put a hand on Ashley's shoulder.

"I liked you the minute I came in here," Ashley continued, turning sad eyes to Kathryn once more. "You listened to me, and really believed me when I said I was marrying Jarrett. You didn't laugh when I said I loved him."

"And I'm not laughing now."

"And when you talked us out of eloping, you didn't say all the trite things everyone else has said. You just told us it was worth waiting to have a real ceremony, worth starting off on the right foot."

"I was sincere in everything I said that morning. If you plan to marry, you should do it the right way, not on the run, not surrounded by strangers."

"I believed all of that," Ashley said. "But I know

Gray is working on you. He thinks you can influence me. I keep waiting for you to say something negative, to try to talk me out of this.''

"So that's why you've been giving me those suspicious looks. I thought it was because you didn't like my dating Gray.''

This time it was Ashley who blinked. She cleared her throat. "Dating?''

The young woman's expression startled Kathryn into silence. Ashley was preoccupied these days, but didn't she see what was going on?

"I know you've been over to dinner,'' Ashley murmured, frowning. "I was there.''

"We've been to the movies, and for long drives, and a concert...'' Kathryn realized Ashley had been so caught up in her own world that she had ignored what was happening between Gray and Kathryn. But how was that possible? "Ashley, you walked in on us the first time your brother kissed me. I see him every day. What did you think was going on?''

Ashley looked uncomfortable. "I guess I didn't think much about it at all.''

"You're kidding.'' An amazed chuckle eased from Kathryn. "Here I've been worrying about what you thought of that kiss, wondering if that was why you were acting so strange.''

"I thought...'' Ashley swallowed. "I thought maybe Gray was trying to win you over to his camp.''

Kathryn laughed some more. "Gee, Ashley, how flattering.''

"What do you mean?''

"It's not exactly complimentary that you thought Gray was only seeing me because of how I might influence you.''

Ashley's face colored. "Oh, gosh, Kathryn, I'm sorry. I didn't mean…it's just that I thought…" Looking miserable, she sank onto the stool in front of the dressing mirror. "Boy, do I feel stupid."

Kathryn patted her on the knee. "You've just got a lot on your mind."

"But you'd think I'd realize…" Ashley shook her head, then straightened and stared at Kathryn. "You and Gray?"

Feeling uncomfortable again, Kathryn bit her lip. "What do you think?"

"You and Gray," Ashley repeated.

"Is it that hard to imagine?"

"Not because of you. But Gray. He's so…"

"Handsome?" Kathryn supplied. "Intelligent. Interesting."

Ashley laughed. "I was going to say stubborn, bull-headed and narrow-minded."

"I must confess, that was my first impression of him. And I believe he can be all of those things at times, the same way as most people. But now…" Thinking of the past few weeks with Gray, Kathryn sighed. They'd spent so much time together. Much of it spent just talking. About their individual plans and dreams. About mundane matters. The sexual fire that had threatened to blaze out of control between them was smoldering, as well, working itself up to a blaze. She was rather enjoying the slow burn. The kisses, the teasing touches, the controlled passion. Those thoughts made her face flame.

Ashley looked astounded. "You're falling for him."

Kathryn gathered her poise. "I like him a great deal," she corrected Ashley. "We have fun together."

"He could use some fun," the younger woman said thoughtfully. "He's never had much time for himself."

"I realize that," Kathryn said. "That's why you should cut him some slack, as well."

Ashley's eyes narrowed. "Uh-oh. Is this the 'why don't you wait to get married' pitch?"

Kathryn shook her head. "I have no right, nor any interest in telling you what to do."

"That's a relief."

"Gray, however, has a lot of interest."

"Interest in controlling me," Ashley said with a sigh.

"Interest in your happiness."

"I'm happy with Jarrett. I just want to marry him, be with him all the time."

The love shining in Ashley's eyes was something Kathryn couldn't dispute. But neither was the worry which she so often heard in Gray's voice when he talked about his sister. Kathryn wanted to bring them together on this subject, to prevent them from breaking their bonds as she had done with her family. She just wasn't sure how to accomplish such a feat. Not yet, anyway.

"What do you think?" Ashley asked her. "About you and Gray?"

Kathryn shrugged. "As I said, I like him."

"And?"

"There's no and."

"Maybe there could be."

"Don't be like Devon." Kathryn shook a warning finger at the younger woman. "Your brother and I are simply enjoying each other's company. That's all either of us wants."

Ashley eyed her with keen speculation for a moment,

"If you say that's all you want, then fine. But I want you to know that it's all cool with me."

"You sure?"

"At least Gray is showing some good sense and taste about something."

Kathryn laughed. "Speaking of your brother," she told Ashley, "he's coming by in a few minutes."

"Then let me out of here."

"Oh, come on. Rick's spending the night with his friend, Tommy, and we're going out to dinner."

"Tommy's is one of the few families that Gray believes can deal with Rick," Ashley said with sarcasm. "He has such *endearing* confidence in both Rick and me."

Kathryn wasn't about to get into another discussion of Gray's protectiveness toward Ashley and her brother, so she went on, "Why not have dinner with me and Gray?"

"Jarrett and I have plans with some friends. We haven't really had too much time together recently."

"What's Jarrett been up to since he got home from school?"

"Working at the ranch all the time. I hardly see him. But next week I'm going to work for Mr. McMullen at the ranch, too." Ashley wrinkled her nose. "I'll be cleaning the guest cottages, but at least I'll be closer to Jarrett."

"Why don't you call him?" Kathryn suggested. "You both could have dinner with me and Gray before you meet your friends."

"And ruin all of our digestions?" Ashley snorted. "No way." Closing the subject firmly, the younger woman turned back to the dresses Kathryn had shown her just a short while ago. She touched the straight-skirted blue gown. "You're right about this dress." She nodded at the fuschia dress. "And about this color."

"You rascal," Kathryn teased. "You were just being difficult because you feared I was going to start telling you to postpone the wedding."

"I was being a brat," Ashley admitted with a sheepish smile. "I'm sorry. You and Devon are doing such a great job with all the plans. I'll bring my bridesmaids by on Monday to see if anyone has any huge objections to this dress."

Nodding, Kathryn scribbled the dress style number and color on a notepad. "I know you want to please your friends, but don't let them influence you too much," she cautioned, slipping her arm around Ashley's shoulders as they moved from the dressing room to the showroom. "This is *your* wedding."

"And Jarrett's," a youngster's voice added.

Kathryn looked up to find Rick standing by Gray's side just outside the curtained dressing-room entrance. Rick was grinning. Gray's expression was borderline grim.

With a toss of her blond hair and not a word for her older brother, Ashley greeted Rick. "You're right, Short-stuff. This is Jarrett's wedding, too. And he told me last night that we have to have you as our ring bearer."

Rick's eyes widened. He turned to Kathryn. "Will you show me what to do?"

"Sure." Kathryn fondly ruffled his hair. "If you want, we can look at some tuxedos for you to wear right now."

"Cool," the boy approved.

"Some other time," Gray said abruptly.

Kathryn saw Ashley's jaw set.

"Why not now?" the younger woman challenged Gray. "I want Rick in the wedding, of course. And I know it's never too early to get things like tuxedos ordered."

Gray looked more determined than ever. "I just think it can wait."

Stepping forward before a famous Ashley-Gray argument could ensue, Kathryn said calmly, "Just for fun, why don't we go through some samples of tuxedo styles. Rick's will have to match Jarrett's, of course, but it's not too early to get some ideas." As she turned Ashley and Rick toward the front of the shop, she looked back at Gray, silently pleading with him to try to meet his sister halfway about something.

Gray saw what Kathryn was thinking. He also saw the arm she had around Rick's shoulders and the easy way she dealt with Ashley. Kathryn had slipped quickly and easily into the lives of his brother and sister.

Into his life, as well, he admitted with reluctance.

He wasn't sure why he was hesitant to acknowledge how big a role Kathryn had assumed in his day-to-day life. After all, he was the one who called her every day, who made it a point to bring lunch by the shop or take her to dinner, who took her to Rick's Little League games and Ashley's graduation and the symphony-in-the-park concert on Sunday afternoon. They were together every day.

Hell, last night he had taken her to look at paint samples for the kitchen walls he was planning to tackle this weekend. With Rick in tow, they had mused over colors and wallpaper samples. It was all very domestic. All very nice. And not what Gray had planned when he started this little adventure with Kathryn. He had envisioned some laughs, which they'd had. And some hot sex, which they were working toward. But he hadn't counted on the way she was becoming entangled in every aspect of his life. This was turning out to be very different from the simple affair he had promised himself.

He should have known. Nothing in his life was easy. Yet he had so wanted his relationship with Kathryn to be uncomplicated. Smothering a groan, he reminded himself that *relationship* and *uncomplicated* were two words that didn't belong in the same sentence.

So what was he going to do? Stop seeing her? He strongly resisted that idea. Damn it, why couldn't he just have some fun? Other men and women did. He should just separate Kathryn from the other parts of his life. He should sleep with her, purge her from his system and then go on.

Having made that determination, Gray turned toward the front of the shop again. But his resolve wavered when he contemplated the happy little group huddled together near the desk. He decided to leave them alone for a moment more, to give himself a chance to collect his thoughts. If he interrupted now, his sister would have a fit, and he really wasn't up for a fight with Ashley. He was weary of their arguing. He moved over to the shop's bay window, where a love seat and chairs were grouped around a low, round table.

Gray sprawled down in one of the well-cushioned chairs and looked for something to keep his mind off his problems. Magazines were spread across the table in front of him, each colorful cover featuring a beautiful bride. Gray scooped up a copy and leafed through it idly, and was soon studying the advertisements and layouts with surprising interest. There wasn't a model pictured who could rival the way Ashley had looked in the gown she had been wearing the first day he had burst into this shop. He wished he could tell her that, wished he could feel good about her plans. Kathryn kept warning him about pushing Ashley away, but how could he give his blessing to a wedding he hated even thinking of?

A burst of laughter drew his attention to the front of the shop. Rick, suited up in a black tuxedo jacket that reached his calves, was doing a penguin walk while Kathryn and Ashley looked on, applauding. Gray started to call out for Rick to settle down, but he bit his lip. Just last night, Kathryn had pointed out again, ever so gently, that he was always anticipating a disaster around Rick. Gray knew she was right, and he was trying to do better, but...

With a muffled curse, Gray tossed the magazine aside. He didn't need Kathryn or anyone else telling him what to do with Rick or Ashley. He had done the best he could for seven years now. He didn't need or want anyone's help. Outsiders had inevitably meant trouble to Gray. From the men who had drifted in and out of his and his mother's life to the fiancée who had left him. Gray knew better than to let anyone get close. He and Kathryn were supposed to be having a light-hearted affair, not getting enmeshed in family ties. To avoid complications, he knew to keep it simple.

He walked to the front of the store. "I hate to interrupt this," he said, carefully keeping his tone as neutral as possible, "but Rick's expected over at his friend Tommy's, and I'm starving."

"I have to go, too." Ashley's laughter faded as she darted Gray an unreadable glance. "You remember that I'm staying the night with Janey, don't you? If you just can't stand the suspense, you can call us up at midnight and see that we're home safe and sound."

He resisted the urge to rise to her bait. "You need some cash?" he asked.

"No, but thanks." A surprising near smile trembled just at the edges of her mouth as she looked at him. Then she turned and said goodbye to Kathryn and Rick.

When she reached the door, old habits overcame Gray, and he said, "Be careful, okay?"

Her answer was a flip of her blond hair. Gray sighed and watched the door close behind her.

But Kathryn, who was standing beside him, squeezed his arm and whispered, "That was a very nice effort on your part."

"She hates me."

"She won't forever." Kathryn faced him, slipping her arms around his waist. "She really loves you a lot."

"Yeah, right." Gray forced his thoughts away from his rebellious sister and onto the gorgeous woman in front of him. Holding her was what he wanted to think about when they were together. All this other stuff was a complicated distraction that had nothing to do with her.

She smiled up at him, her voice slipping into a husky, provocative tone. "Did I hear you say you were hungry?"

"For many things," he murmured, lowering his mouth toward hers.

Rick interrupted the kiss before it could happen with a loud "I'm starved, too."

Heaving a disappointed but good-natured sigh, Gray turned to his brother. He was dismayed to discover that in the few moments he and Kathryn had been concentrating on each other, the boy had managed to pull three more tuxedo jackets from the low-to-the-floor rack of samples behind them.

"Now look here, partner," Gray protested, bending down to retrieve the jackets from the floor, "you know not to throw clothes around like this. Especially clothes that don't belong to you."

"It's no big deal," Kathryn said, chucking the boy under the chin. "You just wanted our attention, didn't you?"

"I want some dinner," Rick said bluntly.

Gray frowned at him. "You're eating at Tommy's, and we'll be on our way in a minute." He held out a hanger and a jacket. "Help put this stuff away."

Rick's answer was a glower. Gray started to reprimand him.

Kathryn took the hanger and made an excuse for Rick. "I think we had better get some food into this young fellow."

"Can I go to dinner with you guys?" Rick asked.

"No," Gray told him. "Tommy's expecting you."

"You'll have more fun with him anyway," Kathryn added.

Rick didn't look convinced. "I think I'd rather go with you."

Kathryn seemed ready to capitulate, but Gray wasn't about to let her. Most of their time together had been spent with Rick as a third wheel. Not tonight. Gray had other, more intimate plans for this evening.

"You're going to Tommy's, just as you've been begging me to do since last weekend." Gray sent a remonstrating glance at Kathryn. "Now let's get a move on."

Storm clouds seemed to gather over Rick's head during the drive to Tommy's, and once there he didn't greet his friend with his normal enthusiasm. Gray felt it only right to warn Tommy's parents that Rick was in a petulant, uncooperative mood.

Tommy's personable father and mother, Stan and Mary Green, had five active boys of their own, and Gray trusted and liked them. Gray hadn't made too many friends since moving to Amarillo, but the Greens had repeatedly reached out to him and to Rick. The counselor at Rick's school had put them in touch. Not only was Mary a child psychologist, but her oldest boy, the product of a first marriage, had some of the same emotional problems that Rick faced. Mary, more than most people Gray had met, seemed to understand what Rick needed in the way of discipline and affection. She and Stan also could identify with Gray's frequent feelings of frustration.

Tonight, Mary seemed especially pleased to see Gray with Kathryn. She told them both to have a wonderful evening and not to worry about Rick, even if the child was in one of his recalcitrant moods. She reminded Gray she'd handled Rick before. So Gray left, feeling his brother was in capable hands.

"You really think he's okay?" Kathryn asked as the Jeep pulled away from the pleasant, two-story house where Rick was still standing in the front yard.

Gray said, "He loves it at Tommy's. There are two older boys to follow around, and two younger boys for him and Tommy to terrorize. It's an eight-year-old boy's dream, and he'll forget about us the minute the Jeep's out of sight."

"If you say so."

Gray removed one hand from the steering wheel and

touched her arm. "Could you forget my brother and concentrate on me?"

Smiling, she covered his hand with her own. "I might. But he is an appealing young man, you know."

"Some people say the same about me."

"Like who?" she replied, playing along with his teasing mood.

"Well, this afternoon, there was this cow with an infected udder—"

"Gray!"

"I swear, Kathryn, she seemed to adore me, kept batting her big brown eyes my way."

"So you prefer brown-eyed girls, huh?"

"Nah." He grinned and turned the Jeep south. "I prefer green eyes. Cat's eyes."

She grimaced. "That's what my brother called me when I was small. Kat, short for Kathryn."

"And it didn't stick?"

"My mother preferred that Luke use my proper name." Without thinking, Kathryn realized she had assumed a haughty, stiff enunciation, much like her mother's normal tone. "Mother also insists on cloth napkins at every meal, pressed sheets on the beds and a purging of all closets at least once every three months."

"She sounds like fun," Gray commented dryly.

Kathryn shrugged, not eager to get into a discussion about Christine Seeger.

Gray added, "I didn't know you had a brother."

"He's older."

"And not close?"

"No."

"But he used to call you Kat."

"A long, long time ago." Kathryn never let herself

dwell for any length of time on her estranged family. She glanced out the window. "Where are we headed anyway?"

"Canyon," Gray replied, naming a small town about twenty miles south of Amarillo. "I have a feeling the sunset over Palo Duro Canyon's going to be nice to-night."

Nice was an understatement. As the sun set west of the magnificent spires of Palo Duro, the June sky streaked with orange, pink and purple. The beauty was as breathtaking for Kathryn as it had been the first time she visited this area with Paige McMullen. Or maybe this evening the sky was even more magnificent. Because Gray was there to appreciate it with her.

He had packed a picnic. Nothing grand. Just chicken and pasta salad from a small restaurant Kathryn favored near her shop. He had also remembered the double fudge brownie she always ordered. It was a small gesture, but thoughtful and touching nonetheless.

They ate near the rim of the canyon, at one of the many picnic tables scattered throughout the area. After dinner, they remained, holding hands, enjoying the fading sunset and talking about the most mundane of matters. Not about families. Or weddings. Or anything too personal. The feeling of intimacy growing between them had more to do with their clasped hands and the looks they exchanged than with anything they said to one another.

And when the hand-holding and the lingering looks weren't enough, kisses were the next logical progression. They started out slow, then grew more heated. Until even a kiss wasn't enough. As twilight fell, Kathryn wound up on the picnic table's bench, on Gray's lap, her body straining against his. She wanted her hands on him, his hands on her. But she wasn't so sure she wanted what they were heading toward to happen on the picnic table or in the back of his Jeep. At any moment, she was expecting a park ranger to appear out of nowhere to shine a light in their eyes and demand that they break it up.

When she confessed her apprehension to Gray, he laughed and undid the final button on her blouse.

"You have no fear," she murmured, the words ending on a sigh as his fingers traced over her budded nipples.

"Not true." Gray nuzzled her neck, the faint stubble on his jaw pleasantly rough against her skin. "I'm actually scared to death."

"Of what?"

"This." His hand cupped the back of her neck as he looked down at her.

She laughed, thinking he was joking. "You don't act so terribly frightened." He was silent, and she realized that he wasn't teasing. "Gray?" she murmured, touching a hand to his cheek. "What is it?"

He exhaled, shaking his head. "I'm a crazy man, you know. I mean, this feels so right." His voice deepened. "And I want you so much...."

She drew his face close to hers, whispering against his lips, "And I want you."

"But I feel like we should be clear about a few things."

"Like what?"

"Like I don't just do this."

Kathryn was silent, not sure what he meant.

"I'm not one of those guys who's casual about who he sleeps with," Gray explained. "Quite frankly, with the kids around most of the time, I never had that kind of freedom or that inclination."

"I'm not casual about it, either." She frowned. "Isn't that why we decided to get to know one another before we got to this point again?"

"Yes, but even though I don't take this lightly, I'm also not..." His gaze shifted away from hers. "I'm not looking for a commitment, Kathryn."

She had known that, of course. She wasn't looking for a commitment, either. So why did his statement make her feel so hollow inside?

"Don't get me wrong," Gray continued. "I told you when we started seeing each other, I'm attracted to you in a lot of ways. This isn't just about sex. But during the past few weeks we've been together a lot. While we've gotten acquainted, we've also gotten...involved."

She was silent, wondering why he felt such a need to drive that point home every chance he could.

"I just don't want there to be any misunderstandings. This is not...not..." His words faded, a frown creasing his brow.

"Not what?"

He shrugged. "You know what I mean."

She did, certainly. What they were engaged in wasn't anything more than two people enjoying one another's company. Just a few hours ago, Kathryn had claimed to Ashley that having fun with Gray was all she wanted. So there was no reason for this big letdown she was feeling. No reason at all. And damnation, she wasn't about to let any messy emotions tangle up her thinking.

Any relationship she might have with Gray was going to have boundaries. She should be relieved. Didn't

PLAY

SILHOUETTE'S

LUCKY HEARTS

GAME

AND YOU GET

★ **FREE BOOKS**

★ **A FREE GIFT**

★ **AND MUCH MORE**

TURN THE PAGE AND
DEAL YOURSELF IN

PLAY "LUCKY HEARTS" AND GET . . .

★ **Exciting Silhouette Special Edition® novels—FREE**

★ **PLUS a Lovely Simulated Pearl Drop Necklace—FREE**

THEN CONTINUE YOUR LUCKY STREAK WITH A SWEETHEART OF A DEAL

1. Play Lucky Hearts as instructed on the opposite page.

2. Send back this card and you'll receive brand-new Silhouette Special Edition® novels. These books have a cover price of $3.99 each, but they are yours to keep absolutely free.

3. There's no catch. You're under no obligation to buy anything. We charge nothing — ZERO — for your first shipment. And you don't have to make any minimum number of purchases — not even one!

4. The fact is thousands of readers enjoy receiving books by mail from the Silhouette Reader Service. They like the convenience of home delivery…they like getting the best new novels month before they're available in stores…and they love our discount prices!

5. We hope that after receiving your free books you'll want to remain a subscriber. But the choice is yours — to continue or cancel, anytime at all! So why not take us up on our invitation, with no risk of any kind. You'll be glad you did!

NOT ACTUAL SIZE

*This lovely necklace will add glamour to your most elegant outfit! Its cobra-link chain is a generous 18" long, and its lustrous simulated cultured pearl is mounted in an attractive pendant! Best of all, it's **absolutely free**, just for accepting our no-risk offer.*

SILHOUETTE'S

With a coin— scratch off the silver card and check below to see what we have for you.

YES! I have scratched off the silver card. Please send me all the free books and gift for which I qualify. I understand that I am under no obligation to purchase any books, as explained on the back and on the opposite page.

235 CIS A7DZ (U-SIL-SE-03/97)

NAME

ADDRESS   APT.

CITY   STATE   ZIP

Twenty-one gets you 4 free books, and a free simulated pearl drop necklace

Twenty gets you 4 free books

Nineteen gets you 3 free books

Eighteen gets you 2 free books

Offer limited to one per household and not valid to current Silhouette Special Edition® subscribers. All orders subject to approval.

© 1990 HARLEQUIN ENTERPRISES LIMITED.   PRINTED IN U.S.A.

DETACH AND MAIL CARD TODAY

THE SILHOUETTE READER SERVICE™: HERE'S HOW IT WORKS

Accepting free books places you under no obligation to buy anything. You may keep the books and gift and return the shipping statement marked "cancel". If you do not cancel, about a month later we'll send you 6 additional novels, and bill you just $3.34 each plus 25¢ delivery per book and applicable sales tax, if any.* That's the complete price–and compared to cover prices of $3.99 each–quite a bargain! You may cancel at any time, but if you choose to continue, every month we'll send you 6 more books, which you may either purchase at the discount price…or return to us and cancel your subscription.

*Terms and prices subject to change without notice. Sales tax applicable in N.Y.

If offer card is missing, write to: Silhouette Reader Service, 3010 Walden Ave, P.O. Box 1867, Buffalo, NY 14240-1867

BUSINESS REPLY MAIL
FIRST-CLASS MAIL   PERMIT NO. 717   BUFFALO, NY

POSTAGE WILL BE PAID BY ADDRESSEE

SILHOUETTE READER SERVICE
3010 WALDEN AVE
PO BOX 1867
BUFFALO NY 14240-9952

NO POSTAGE
NECESSARY
IF MAILED
IN THE
UNITED STATES

she like limits, *control?* What Gray was offering was exactly the sort of relationship she wanted—no ties, no promises. She wasn't interested in turning her life over to someone else, placing her happiness in a man's hands. She had gone that route. But that was no reason to be lonely, no reason to forgo the pleasure of Gray's company, the strength of his arms, the completion she knew she would find when they made love. There was no reason, in fact, for them to be wasting time talking about commitments. That wasn't what she wanted.

"Kiss me," she abruptly instructed him.

He looked startled.

"Don't think about it. Just kiss me, Gray. And then let's get in the Jeep and head back to my place. And let's make love all night long."

He continued to stare at her, clearly amazed, but as she met his gaze head-on, a smile curved his mouth. "I have to tell you, Miss Seeger, you are some kind of woman."

"A brazen hussy?"

"I like my women forward," he said, finally obeying her command to kiss her.

"Your *women?*" she said, breaking away. "I thought you said there hadn't been so many."

He grinned. "Uh-oh. Caught me, didn't you?"

"Well…" Kathryn twisted around so that he was leaning back against the tabletop and she was straddling his lean hips. She rotated her hips downward in a bold, suggestive motion. "I haven't caught you," she whispered. "Not yet anyway." Where their bodies pressed so intimately together, Kathryn could feel Gray's sex hardening. She wiggled against him again.

He groaned. "Don't do that unless you mean it."

"You've got a deal. But you've got to take me home."

"It's a long drive. Are you sure you can wait?"

"It'll give us time to build the anticipation."

Gray chuckled. "Seems to me that's already been accomplished." But he sat up, set Kathryn reluctantly away and helped her straighten her clothing. Within minutes, they had gathered up the remains of their picnic and were headed north to Amarillo.

Night had fallen. The air was clear and cool, and a breeze lifted Kathryn's hair as they sped along the highway. Gray held her hand tightly. They made little attempt at conversation. Every once in a while, she glanced his way. The lights from passing cars highlighted his clean-cut profile. And often, he looked at her and smiled. She kept thinking of his kiss and his touch, of the mutual pleasure tonight would hold. The current of awareness strengthened between them, so intense that her breath quickened. She resisted the urge to tell Gray to drive faster.

On the outskirts of town, his cellular telephone rang. Kathryn jumped, staring at the contraption like an unwelcome intruder. Which it was, of course.

Gray snapped the slim phone open with practiced ease. "It's probably my service," he said. "Some rancher probably needs me early tomorrow morning."

Kathryn nodded, praying it wasn't someone who would request his services right now. Surely no one could need him more than she did tonight.

But someone did.

Rick.

Chapter Six

Mary Green met Gray's Jeep at the curb in front of her home. She was wringing her hands, full of apologies.

"I'm so sorry to call and interrupt your evening," the plump, pretty blonde said, looking from Gray to Kathryn as she led them up the front walk and into the house. "But Rick's had a bad time tonight. I just couldn't do anything with him. I knew you'd want to be called, Gray."

"I'm the one who's sorry," Gray replied, feeling guilty. "I knew he was working up to one of his tantrums. I never should have left him tonight."

Mary directed them through a comfortably messy living room and out a set of French doors to the backyard. "Now just stop it, Gray. You know I'm fond of Rick, and you know I'm usually able to deal with him."

"What happened?" Kathryn asked.

Quickly, Mary explained that Rick had been inconsolable after Gray and Kathryn left. He had calmed down somewhat to eat dinner and play with Tommy. Then he had asked for Gray again. He had grown increasingly upset when Mary refused to call Gray. By this time, Tommy had lost patience with him. The two little boys had a tussle, and Rick had gone out to hide in the play fort in the backyard. He'd refused entreaties and bribes by all of the Greens to come down and had alternated between angry outbursts and sobs. He didn't want anyone, not even Mary, near him to offer comfort.

Rick was crying now, Gray realized as they approached the fort. Nodding to Stan and Tommy, who were standing at the base of the structure, he climbed up the ladder, squeezing through the kid-size portal into the covered platform at the top. The ceiling was so low that Gray had to kneel, but at least he could see. A flashlight had been placed in the fort, no doubt by Mary or Stan, who wouldn't want Rick up here in the dark. The lamp's beam cast eerie shadows throughout the space, highlighting the small figure huddled in one corner.

"What's all this?" Gray asked his brother.

Rick's sobs quieted somewhat, but he didn't look up. "Go away."

"But Mary said you wanted me to come and get you."

"No."

From past experience, Gray knew Rick was feeling embarrassed about the ruckus he had caused. Remorse always followed his storms. "Hey, it's no big deal. I don't mind coming to get you."

Rick's only answer was a ragged sigh.

"Come on." Gray put out his hand. "Let's go home. We can talk about what upset you tomorrow."

"I'll stay here."

"Now come on," Gray said, letting his tone grow sterner. "It's time to be a big guy and come down from here."

Rick pressed his face into the rough-hewn board wall. "Don't want to."

Gray sighed, seeing this was going to be difficult. He was about to speak again, to offer more reassurance, when he heard a sound on the ladder. He twisted around just as Kathryn's head appeared through the doorway.

"Rick?" she said, coming into the cramped space.

Frowning, Gray said, "It's okay, Kathryn. He'll be fine."

"But I was worried." She turned to the boy. "What's wrong, kiddo? Did you miss Gray?"

Rick, not looking at her, gave a barely perceptible nod.

"Well, he's here now."

Finally, the small boy turned to face her.

"I'm here, too. We came to take you home."

Again, Gray put out his hand. "That's right. Let's go home."

The flashlight's beam revealed fresh tears filling the boy's eyes. "I'm sorry."

"About what?" Kathryn soothed, scooting closer to him.

"I'm sorry Mary called you. I'm sorry I was bad." The tears overflowed again.

"Oh, sweetie." Kathryn crawled over beside the boy. Surprising Gray, Rick didn't resist when she wrapped her arms around him. "You weren't bad."

Rick pressed his face against her chest, crying softly. "I got scared."

"We all get scared," Kathryn assured him.

"Tommy said I was a baby."

"He was just teasing."

"He made me mad."

Kathryn laid her cheek against the boy's blond hair. "I'm sure he didn't mean to hurt your feelings. You can make up with him tomorrow."

With soothing words, hugs and kisses, she soon quieted Rick's tears. Gray remained off to the side, surprised at the way Kathryn handled the situation and filled with another emotion he couldn't quite describe. But there was no time to analyze his feelings now. Gray and Kathryn were soon able to convince Rick to go home. All three of them climbed down from the fort.

Only Mary was on the ground to greet them. She had wisely sent Tommy and Stan into the house. Rick was so ashamed of himself that he hid his face against Kathryn's side instead of looking at Mary. Gray saw his own amazement mirrored in Mary's expression. Next to Gray and Ashley, Mary had become Rick's port in a storm this past year. But in a few short weeks, Kathryn had assumed a place of importance in his affections. He knew Rick liked her, wanted to be with her, but the relationship that had grown between them was far greater than Gray had imagined. Mary was beaming approval. Gray wasn't sure how he felt.

In the Jeep, Gray told Rick, "We'll head for home as soon as I drop Kathryn off."

The youngster, who had insisted on squeezing into the front passenger seat with Kathryn, protested, "Can't she come home with us, too?"

"No, now—"

"Please?" the boy pressed.

"I don't mind," Kathryn said quickly.

Gray acquiesced. God knew, they didn't need any more tantrums tonight. He would worry about getting Kathryn home after Rick was settled for the night.

That task proved relatively easy. Rick let Gray help him brush his teeth and get into his pajamas. But it was Kathryn he wanted to tuck him into bed. Kathryn whom he asked to hear his prayers. And Kathryn he asked to sit beside him while he tried to go to sleep.

Gray hovered in the doorway to his brother's room until he was certain the child was headed toward slumber. He left Kathryn still holding him and went to the kitchen. He felt the same weariness he usually experienced after dealing with one of Rick's episodes. Added to that was the guilt he had over leaving the boy in the first place when he had seen the warning signs. And then there were his feelings toward Kathryn—a mixture of regret and despair.

She came into the kitchen just as Gray was pouring himself a cup of coffee. "I could use one of those," she said.

Silently, he filled a mug and handed it to her.

She took a long, satisfying sip. "Rick's out for the night, I hope. He was completely exhausted."

Gray nodded, hoping she was right. "You can take my Jeep and go home. I'll wait till Ashley gets home in the morning, and then we'll pick the Jeep up at your shop."

Kathryn hesitated, her gaze uncertain. "I could stay."

He turned away. "No, Kathryn, really..."

"But Rick may wake up, get upset again—"

"I can take care of that. I've had plenty of practice."

She was silent while Gray busied himself putting the coffee can and filters away, wiping off the counter, doing anything but looking at her.

"I guess I now know what you've tried to explain to me about Rick," she said finally.

"He sometimes gets upset when I leave him," Gray said, keeping his tone matter-of-fact. "Hard as I've tried to make him feel secure, I made some mistakes when he was younger. I left him too much. And now he panics, thinks I'm not coming back, then he's ashamed of his reactions."

"Gray," Kathryn protested, "I would venture a guess that any child, losing both parents like he did, would have some issues to deal with, some problems."

Gray shrugged and refilled his coffee mug. "He didn't have other parents long enough for that to be a real issue. His problems are my fault. In the beginning I was young, unprepared."

"Stop being so hard on yourself." Stepping closer, Kathryn took hold of his arm. "When you went up to get him out of that fort tonight, Mary Green told me how much she thought of you and what a terrific job you've done with Rick since moving here."

Setting his mug on the counter, Gray faced her. "Rick is improving, but sometimes his emotional needs can still be overwhelming."

Kathryn put her own coffee aside and slipped her arms around his waist. "I can't imagine how you've managed so well with all you've been through."

Her embrace felt so good, her soft voice was so comforting, that for a moment Gray forgot himself. He let himself give in to her tender succor. Putting his arms around her, he leaned against her strong but slender frame. It wasn't easy to accept her comfort. Gray hadn't been able to count on many people in his life, so he had learned not to expect support. But for now he enjoyed what Kathryn was offering.

Against her silky, fragrant hair, he whispered, "This isn't what I planned for tonight."

"Oh, I don't know." Kathryn drew back, her fingers sliding to the front of his cotton shirt, where she unbuttoned a button. "I figured we'd be in each other's arms right about now."

"I'm talking about our dealing with an eight-year-old's panic attack."

She undid another button. "Rick's problems tonight don't change how much I want you. And he's fast asleep. And Ashley's gone...." The smile she angled his way was full of wicked, sexy intent as still another button was released.

Gray's hands covered hers, stilling her actions. He wished Rick hadn't picked tonight to have "problems," as Kathryn so gently put it. And yet Gray figured this was inevitable. All his plans for separating Kathryn from the rest of his complicated life were ridiculous. He had known that from the start, but he had plunged ahead with this relationship, hoping for the best. What a fool he was.

Kathryn tipped her head to the side. "You look entirely too serious for a man who promised to make love to me all night long."

"Serious is my normal state, I'm afraid. I'm not a fun and games kind of guy. I shouldn't pretend otherwise."

She studied him for a moment. "Don't pull back from me, Gray."

"I'm not." The lie leaped quickly to his lips. But he knew he had to correct it. "Maybe I am."

"Because of tonight with Rick?"

"Yes."

"But why?"

"Because I can't really give you what I promised."

She stepped away, leaning back against the counter. "I don't understand."

"There's just too much going on in my life right now, Kathryn. There's always too much going on. I have no business getting involved—even casually— with you or anyone else."

"I don't see why."

"Because I already belong to Rick. To Ashley." He grimaced. "Even if she really does marry Jarrett, she'll still be my little sister, the one who's always wading in over her head and getting her heart broken. Something tells me she will need me more than ever if the wedding comes off as planned. And Rick...well, the little guy needs all my extra time and attention."

Kathryn was silent, watching him with big, sad eyes. "What does any of that have to do with me?"

"That's just it." Frustrated, Gray thrust his hands into his jeans pockets. "None of this should have anything to do with you. But unlike some men who have total responsibility for their families, I don't get much downtime. There isn't some nice grandmother out there to help me. There aren't even too many friends I can count on. Right now, I can't plan a romantic evening without the fear that Rick is going to need me. And that means I don't have time for you. For us."

"After getting to know me these past few weeks, do I strike you as the kind of person who would resent your devoting time to Ashley and Rick?"

"Not now," Gray said. "But later..."

"This isn't later." Pointing emphatically at the floor, she said, "This is where we are right now. And I'm willing to share you."

Gray closed his eyes. This seemed so familiar. His ex-fiancée had made the same claims. But his family situation had eventually overwhelmed her, driven her away. Her defection had hurt him deeply. His and Kathryn's relationship couldn't begin to compare with an engagement. But Kathryn was still a complication he didn't need, and it was better to put on the brakes once and for all.

"I'm sorry," he told her. "I just don't want to mislead you."

"That's what you keep saying," Kathryn murmured, lifting her chin. "But I don't much believe you."

He assumed a defensive pose, feet braced wide apart, arms crossed.

"You're lying as much to yourself as to me. And you shouldn't lie, Gray. You're not very good at it."

"What are you talking about?"

"It's obvious," she retorted. "You're not dealing with the real issues here. You won't admit that you're afraid of letting me get close."

But that was exactly what he feared. Hoping to cover that truth, Gray glared at her.

Hands on her slim hips, Kathryn paced away from him. "You've got a big problem, Gray. You're very impressed with yourself."

"What?"

"That's right." She whirled to face him again. "You've played the big, responsible male for so damn long. You know you do it well, and you don't want to give it up. You don't know how to let go of any of that responsibility. That's what's wrong between you and Ashley. And eventually it'll come between you and Rick. Most certainly, it's going to interfere with any woman you might try to have a relationship with."

He held up a hand to stop her. "You've missed the whole point of everything I've said to you."

"Because everything you've said is bull."

"Oh, please." With a dismissive wave, he turned away, determined to find his car keys and get her out of here.

But Kathryn stopped him by taking firm hold of his arm. "You need to hear this, Gray. You need to face the fact that you sort of like having to be the strong one all the time. You don't want to share anything with anyone for fear your burden will lighten. Hell, you were jealous tonight when I was the one who calmed Rick down."

She was right. Jealousy was exactly the elusive emotion he had tried to name when she was the one to calm Rick down. But he wasn't about to admit to that. "That's ridiculous."

"You were so surprised that anyone else could reach him. Surprised and maybe a little bit disappointed, as well. You're so used to being his everything."

"You don't know what you're talking about. I welcome anyone, you or Mary Green or Ashley or a teacher, anyone who can help Rick."

"But letting go is like pulling teeth, isn't it?"

Damn, but she could see his every feeling. He hated that. "You're way off base."

"I know what I see," she insisted, her voice softening. "And I see a guy who could use a hand."

His frown deepened. "So this is pity you're offering

me now? Some tea and sympathy, and a little roll in the hay on the side?''

Kathryn chose to ignore his crudeness. ''Tell me what's wrong with a little sympathy, a little help?''

''I didn't ask for it.''

''That's when it's easiest to give.''

The four-letter word he uttered was direct and to the point. Turning to the counter again, he picked up the car keys. ''Let's stop this now, Kathryn. You go home. I'll get the Jeep tomorrow. We'll both look at the past couple of weeks as just a mistake, all right?'' He held out the keys. ''It's been nice knowing you.''

''So you're throwing me out?''

''I think you should go, yes.''

''What if I don't want to go? What if I stand here until you give me some real answers about why you're giving up on us before we even get started?''

Groaning, Gray flung the keys aside again. He thrust his face close to hers. His clear blue eyes glittered dangerously. ''We aren't right for each other. You don't have a clue what my life is like.''

She matched him glare for glare. ''God in heaven, do you think you're the only person who has a complicated life?''

His laugh was short. ''And just what do you have to contend with, Miss Seeger?''

''A business,'' she retorted. ''And friends...and...'' Her face flamed as the list faltered. She could have told him about disappointments, regrets, about the child she had lost. But all of that was in her past.

Gray looked victorious. ''You see. Our realities are so far apart that it's almost funny. You've got this nice, straightforward life, and I've got one long, extended crisis.''

In some respects he was right, Kathryn thought. She didn't have many immediate complications in her life. She had structured it that way deliberately. When she got away from Darren, away from her mother, away from all the heartbreak and sadness she had known in her marriage and immediately thereafter, she had carefully shut herself off from the possibility of more turmoil. She had pretended to be happy, fulfilled, content. But lately…

Lately? Oh, hell, she might as well admit the truth. Ever since Gray came stomping into her shop looking for Ashley, Kathryn had been questioning the choices she had made. A yearning had started deep inside her. The feeling was complex, wrapped up in sexual attraction, tied off with a deep need for family, a need she had tried to bury. That hankering had begun with Ashley's asking her for comfort and reassurance. It grew each time a certain little boy slipped his hand in hers. And the need flourished under something as simple as a smile from the stubborn man who faced her now with such anger on his face.

Kathryn knew she was on dangerous ground. She could fall for this man, fall very hard for someone who contended he didn't want her in his life at all. A stubborn, prideful man, who hadn't the slightest clue about how to share his life, his problems and joys, with someone else. All her fine resolutions earlier this evening about not wanting a commitment dissipated like so much dust. She wanted much more than a few nights with Gray, much more than he had offered thus far. And that want was a prescription for disaster.

Yet the worst medicine she could imagine would be walking out that door.

Drawing in a deep, calming breath, she decided to

bet on what she knew to be one of Gray's best qualities. He was completely, absolutely honest. She could see through any lie he might tell her.

"Let me make you a deal," she said, finally breaking the silence that had fallen between them.

"About what?"

"Just listen. And look at me."

"Kathryn..."

She moved forward, taking hold of his arms once more, all but forcing him to look down at her. She gazed into his clear blue eyes and spoke calmly. "I want you to tell me to go away, Gray."

Shrugging, he looked away. "That's easy."

"No," she said, holding tight to him. "That's not how I want you to do it. I want you to look at me and tell me you really don't want to pursue what we've started."

"All right," he agreed, looking at her again.

Her eyes didn't waver from his regard. "Tell me," she murmured. "Look at me and tell me to leave, to not come back. Tell me you don't care if you ever see me again."

Gray frowned. "Kathryn, this is silly."

"Say it," she insisted. "Say it and mean it, and I'll go. I'll go and take all my accusations with me."

"Accusations?" he repeated, a vertical crease appearing between his eyebrows again.

"I'll take back everything I said about your needing someone."

Muscles worked in his throat. "I want you to go."

His voice held no conviction. Kathryn said, "I don't believe you."

Blinking, he tried again. "I don't need you. I don't...want..." The assertion fell apart completely as his gaze faltered beneath hers. He squeezed his eyes shut. "I don't want you in my life."

"You didn't look at me when you said that."

His eyes opened, though he still didn't look at her again. "Hellfire, Kathryn. Stop being ridiculous."

"Just do it. Look at me and say it like you really mean it, or accept the consequences."

His incredibly blue eyes swung back toward her again. He opened his mouth. He stuttered, "I want... I..."

Triumph began to beat inside her chest. "You can't say it." Her hand slipped down his arms to his hands. As if by rote, his fingers spread and entwined with hers. "You can't say it and mean it, can you?"

Misery clouded his features.

Kathryn began to laugh. "I knew you couldn't look at me and lie."

"That doesn't mean anything. We're still worlds apart, Kathryn."

She moved closer. "Not really."

He lifted a hand to her cheek. "Why in the world do you want to get involved with me? If you were smart you'd run away."

"I did run, remember? The first time you kissed me. But I came back."

"That's when I should have resisted."

"But you didn't. So now you've got to see this through."

With a sigh, he dipped his head toward hers, touching her lips with his mouth with a gentleness that quickly turned to fire. Long moments passed before he drew back, murmuring, "What in the hell are we doing?"

She groaned softly. "Did anyone ever tell you that you have a tendency to overanalyze things?"

"My mother."

"And what did she suggest you do about it?"

"Go with the flow."

"She sounds very wise." Grasping his collar, Kathryn tugged him gently toward her again.

"Going with the flow was how she wound up in all her messes."

Kathryn kissed him in reply. She was tired of the talk, weary of his hesitation, of her own. They were going to be lovers, and whatever came from that action was something they would each have to deal with tomorrow. All she wanted to concentrate on was the here and now. Gray's touch. His kiss. Her reactions. Their mutual pleasure.

As the boundaries and controls in Kathryn's mind were knocked aside by a flood of desire, Gray seemed caught by the same current. Hesitation turned to purpose. Somberness was replaced by freeing laughter. The boyish side of him that she had glimpsed on occasion these past few weeks reappeared with a vengeance.

His quick kisses, light and teasing, gave her no time to rethink what she was about to do. His deep voice, thickened with need, told her what he was going to do to her, what he wanted from her. Like wind in a sail, his breathless, erotic words filled her mind with images, filled her body with impatient need.

Eager hands worked at their clothing. His shirt. Hers. The buckle of his belt. The zipper of his jeans. The front fastening of her bra. The stroke of his tongue replaced the touch of his fingers. Her nipples bloomed under his ministrations. Anticipation became pulsing, liquid excitement deep in her belly. His sex was a hard, growing ridge beneath her palm's exploration.

This wasn't new territory. But the anchor was out of the water. This time they were sailing toward a concrete destination.

Like two impatient kids, they gathered discarded clothing and sneaked hand in hand down the hall past the room where Rick slept. In Gray's room, the door was quickly closed and locked behind them. On his bed, he laid Kathryn down.

Time slowed. They sailed in a lazy circle of escalating need. Gray made a game of undressing her the rest of the way, a sexy frolic of kiss and touch. Kathryn stretched, luxuriating in his easy explorations. She sighed as his lips lingered on her breasts. Giggled as his tongue skimmed across the sensitive skin of her stomach. But the laughter died as his fingers spread across her mound, then dipped lower into the feminine cleft. Instinct took him straight to the kernel of flesh that hardened at his touch. Pleasure moved in waves up her body. Damp with perspiration, craving completion, Kathryn felt her patience reach its end.

Trembling, she pulled away from Gray's blissful massage. She tugged eagerly at the jeans he hadn't shed.

Gray stilled her anxious motions. "Take it easy. We can make it last."

"But I want you inside me. Now."

He rolled away from her, standing beside the bed to shuck his jeans and briefs in one fluid motion. The light from the bedside lamp revealed the hard muscles of his back, the firm planes of his taut buttocks and powerful legs. And when he turned, the soft golden glow caressed his proudly jutting sex.

Murmuring her pleasure, Kathryn sat up and reached out to brush her fingertips across his manhood's hot, velvet tip. The shaft pulsed in response, and Gray groaned. Reveling in his hard, smooth length, anticipating his slide into her welcoming body, Kathryn knelt in front of him. Gray's breath came in ever-shortening gasps as her fingers stroked him, encouraging a need that required no more inspiration.

He stopped her. Voice choking, he said, "Wait right here." Then he disappeared into the bathroom and came back carrying a small, square packet. His laugh was soft and shaky. "I hope to hell this thing isn't too old to do its job."

"Let's hope for the best."

In the dim light, his blue eyes gleamed as his gaze met hers. "It's been a while for me, Kathryn."

"For me, too." Her hand trembled as she took the package from him. At the moment, it felt as if a lifetime had passed since she had been in this situation. Only sex had never felt quite like this. Her young, selfish husband had never volunteered to take care of things, as Gray was so thoughtfully doing. And she couldn't remember ever feeling as she did now, as if she was windsailing over whitecaps. She was shaking so that she couldn't even open the package.

"Let me," Gray murmured, taking over the intimate task.

In moments, she was back in his arms. Kissing, they eased back on the bed. But as her legs slipped apart to receive him, Gray drew back. Their eyes locked as his sex filled her. One stroke. Two. Kathryn stopped counting as her body curved around his, as she matched the rhythm of his thrusts.

All her yearnings, all the needs she had tried to deny,

crystallized as Gray's firm, masculine body moved against her, in her. There was a rightness to this moment, a completeness, that had as much to do with a joining of spirits as of bodies.

The care with which Gray had treated her the past few weeks didn't disappear now. He was taking her, yes. With hard, male plunges driving into her, there was no doubt who was controlling the pace of their intimate pas de deux. But he crooned soft words of encouragement. His hands on her skin were gentle. And as he reached fulfillment, as his body stretched like steel above her own, he smiled and laughed out loud. That gesture, that evidence of his pure, unbridled pleasure in this moment, was what sent Kathryn over the edge. Her breath caught. Her body convulsed. And she looked right into Gray's blue, blue eyes as she sailed over the horizon and into bliss.

The end of one journey. The start of another, much longer passage.

That was the only thought that filled Kathryn's mind as her release faded from intense pleasure to a tranquil thrumming deep inside.

Breathing hard, Gray pulled away and lay on his back beside her. He was floating toward heaven, he thought, as an unstrained, easy silence fell. He felt no compunction to talk, which was strange. He didn't recall ever feeling as though he didn't have to talk to a woman. But then, had there really been any other woman in his life like this one?

Kathryn turned on her side, one leg curving around his. Her chuckle was one of deep satisfaction. "Gray?" she whispered.

"Yeah?" he answered lazily.

"Let's do it again."

He turned, looked into her bright, pretty eyes and began to laugh.

"What's so funny?" she demanded.

"I was just thinking about how I started out believing you were one cool customer."

Her eyes widened, all innocence. "You don't anymore?"

"No, ma'am," he growled, turning to gather her hot, eager body close once again. "And I'm damned glad I was wrong."

Then, as she had so delicately requested, they did it again.

A couple of times.

Chapter Seven

"So...what are your thoughts on a double wedding?"

Ashley's question sent the plate of cookies Kathryn held crashing to the kitchen counter.

The younger woman giggled. "I wish you could see your face."

"If you think my face is in bad shape, you should take my pulse." Kathryn gathered the pieces of her composure together as she began rescuing broken cookies from the counter.

She had spent the first half of this Sunday afternoon contentedly baking chocolate chip cookies for Gray and Rick. After several days of atypical rainy weather, the brothers were taking advantage of the sunshine to work in the small vegetable garden Gray had planted in the yard. Now Ashley, who looked both childlike and very adult in her denim shorts and midriff-baring top, had come home and rattled the peace of the day with her startling question.

And she wasn't through. "You are going to marry Gray, aren't you?"

"Ashley!" Kathryn protested. "What brought this on?"

With a trademark flip of her long blond hair, Ashley said, "All I know is that ever since I got up to speed about this relationship you're having with my brother, I've been noticing just how serious things have become."

Kathryn remained calm, even as her brain raced. After becoming lovers more than a month ago, she and Gray had been carefully discreet around Ashley and Rick. Neither Gray nor Kathryn were ashamed of their deepening relationship, but they also didn't want to confront Rick or Ashley with situations that would make them uncomfortable. If the sly glance Ashley was sending Kathryn's way was any indication, however, the young woman knew a dramatic shift had occurred.

Pretending innocence, Kathryn finished returning unbroken cookies to the plate and reached for a baking sheet to replenish those that had been ruined.

"You might as well tell me the truth." Grinning, Ashley plucked a cookie morsel from the mess on the counter. "I know you guys are sleeping together."

Her suspicion confirmed, Kathryn simply stood, face flaming, unsure of how to reply to Ashley's blunt statement.

"I better take these," Ashley said, rescuing the plate from Kathryn's rather tenuous grip.

"You shouldn't drop bombshells like that," Kathryn told her.

"I'm not disapproving," Ashley said. "Frankly, I'd

be more concerned if you weren't sleeping with him. It just goes to show that Gray is becoming more and more normal. But I do have a question for you.''

Kathryn sent a distracted glance toward the back door, wishing Gray would come inside and rescue her from his sister's inquisition. "I don't think this is a conversation I want to have just now."

"All I want to know is what your intentions are."

"My intentions?"

Ashley set the cookies down and strolled unconcernedly to the refrigerator, from which she took a canned soft drink. "I know Gray," she said matter-of-factly. "He must be madly in love with you if things have gone this far."

"Oh, really?"

"He's not casual about sex."

"Is that so?" Amusement was quickly replacing Kathryn's discomfiture. Ashley was trying so hard to sound so knowing and sophisticated.

"I wouldn't want to see Gray hurt," Ashley continued. "Not like he's been hurt before."

"By his ex-fiancée?"

Now Ashley looked surprised. "He told you about her?"

"Of course." Gray had given Kathryn only perfunctory details about the woman, but that had been enough for her to read between the lines and see how betrayed he had felt when she broke their engagement. Kathryn wouldn't mind a little more information, so she asked Ashley, "What was your take on his fiancée?"

The younger woman popped open the canned drink and shrugged. "She was okay."

"Just okay?"

"It was Gray's fault that they broke up, but it

seemed to me that she could have hung in there a little bit longer.''

Kathryn frowned. ''Gray's fault?'' That hadn't been her impression at all.

But Ashley obviously wasn't much interested in the woman her brother used to be involved with. She returned the focus to Kathryn. ''Gray wouldn't be this involved with you if things weren't pretty serious. So I don't see that my question about a wedding is so out of line.''

''I don't know what you mean by serious. But about the double wedding—don't bet on it.''

''Just because Gray hasn't asked yet doesn't mean it won't happen. If you're in love…''

A big if, Kathryn said to herself, though she didn't want to say it aloud. She busied herself raking cookie crumbs from the counter to the sink. ''Ashley, my dear, Gray and I may be involved, but marriage is not a possibility at this time. And not just because Gray hasn't asked.''

''Oh.'' Frowning, Ashley took a sip from her drink before adding, ''It's always interesting to me that older people like to play the do-as-I-say-not-as-I-do game.''

''What does that mean?''

''Just that Gray would probably go nuts if he knew I was sleeping with Jarrett, even though we're engaged, even though Gray once suggested that very thing himself. And yet it's fine for him to be involved with you, with no wedding in sight. That's a big double standard.''

Which was exactly why we were trying to be discreet. Sighing, Kathryn cast about for an answer, then she realized what Ashley had confessed about herself. Turning to the young woman, a question popped out before Kathryn could give it careful consideration. "So you're sleeping with Jarrett?"

Ashley flushed and lifted her chin.

Kathryn forestalled any explanation with an upheld hand. "I'm sorry, Ashley. That was a personal question I shouldn't have asked."

"But obviously Gray told you we *weren't* sleeping together."

"Well…" Kathryn bit her lip, wishing she had kept her question to herself.

"It's okay," Ashley muttered. "I guess since you're so involved, I should expect him to tell you a lot of stuff."

"He talks about you a lot. Probably because he cares."

With another flip of her hair, Ashley let out a long breath. "Well, as for this…Jarrett came home for the summer, and everything…changed." Her somewhat forlorn expression changed to one of defiance. "We are getting married, you know."

"Yes, you are," Kathryn replied, trying to keep any hint of disapproval out of her voice. For what right did she have to question the choice Ashley had made? Aside from the fact that Gray and Kathryn were, as Ashley put it, *involved* with no wedding in sight, the girl was eighteen years old. No child, she was smart and determined, much more together than Kathryn had been at the same age. At least Kathryn thought she was. But if all was completely right with Ashley, why the troubled set to her mouth?

Ashley was not inviting her interference, but Kathryn plunged ahead anyway. "Is there something wrong?"

"Of course not," the younger woman said, her smile

just a little too forced. "I love Jarrett. Everything's just fine. Especially since Gray has backed off a little bit about the wedding. I know you've had something to do with that. He's easing up a little bit about me and Rick since you've been around."

Kathryn didn't want to take total credit for Gray becoming a little less controlling with his siblings, but she admitted he had made some changes.

"I hope you don't tell Gray about me and Jarrett," Ashley continued. "He'll go ballistic again, and there's nothing to worry about. I've got things under control."

Kathryn wasn't convinced, but she didn't know what else she could say without stepping completely out of the bounds of her relationship with Ashley. She couldn't resist adding, "You will be careful, won't you?"

She didn't blame Ashley for her groan and rolling eyes.

"I know that's what everyone would say to you," Kathryn murmured. "You're no dummy, and I'm sounding like the kind of adult you were just complaining about. But I do care about you. I want you to be happy and safe. So please be careful."

"Yes, well, you and Gray should be careful, too," Ashley answered tartly.

Kathryn's laugh was rueful. "I guess I deserve that, but I'm serious about being concerned for you, Ashley. If there's ever anything you want to talk about, I may not be able to help, but I'm always here."

Looking uncomfortable, Ashley glanced away.

"Gray's here for you, too," Kathryn added, even though she suspected she should back off.

Ashley chewed on her bottom lip for a moment.

"There is something I wouldn't mind a man's perspective on."

Kathryn was fighting the urge to push for details when Gray appeared in the doorway of the utility porch.

"What's up?" he asked with a wide, disarming grin.

Kathryn returned his smile, amazed as always by the way her heart gave a funny little jump when he came into a room. Before Gray, she had never believed reactions like that were possible outside the realm of adolescent crushes. For even in a shirt damp with perspiration and blue jeans splattered with mud, he was a sight that increased her heart rate.

She wasn't so caught up in Gray that she missed the teasing look Ashley darted her way. "Kathryn and I were just discussing weddings," the younger woman told her brother.

Gray grunted a reply. It was true he didn't launch into a furious tirade at the mention of the wedding anymore, but that didn't mean he approved. He plucked a cookie from the plate on the counter and took a bite. "These are great," he said and dropped a kiss on Kathryn's forehead.

His sister cocked her head to the side as she studied them. "You two look very domestic."

Kathryn sent her a warning glance. She didn't know how Gray would react if Ashley started talking about their getting married, and she wasn't sure she wanted to find out. "Where's Rick?" she asked, eager to change subjects.

"Rounding up his new calf." Just yesterday, Gray had presented his younger brother with a calf to raise. Rick had spent every spare moment since with the heifer he had named Sunny.

"Isn't Sunny in the barn?" Ashley asked.

Gray laughed. "Rick told me he thought Sunny was bored."

Kathryn grinned. "How could he tell?"

"Beats me," Gray replied. "But he asked if he could let her out in the pasture for a while. There's nothing wrong with that, except when we got through in the garden, she had wandered out of sight."

Stepping to the corner window that overlooked the back and side yards, Kathryn gazed toward the pasture, but didn't spy Rick or Sunny or the two beagles who were seldom far from the boy's heels. Rick was so enchanted with his calf that she hated to think how he would react if anything happened to her. "Should we go help him look?"

"Of course not," Gray said. "He'll be fine, and so will Sunny. The pasture is fenced, and she couldn't have gone far. She's probably just out by the creek."

Kathryn turned from the window, hoping he was right.

As he picked up two more cookies, Gray said to Ashley, "Strange to see you home on a Sunday afternoon. Where's the boyfriend?" Despite his mellowing attitude, he consistently refused to call Jarrett her fiancé.

With a too-careful lift of one shoulder, Ashley drained the rest of her drink and set the can on the counter.

"Have a fight?" Gray pressed.

Ashley didn't look at him. "Maybe."

"Anything I should celebrate?"

"Gray," Kathryn admonished as she moved back to his side.

To her surprise, Ashley gave no smart retort, didn't

flash her engagement ring or needle him in her usual manner.

Her brother's eyebrows drew together. "You okay?"

"Sure." Ashley headed toward the door. "I think I'll go help Rick."

Gray was silent until the utility porch door slapped shut behind her. "What do you suppose is up with her?"

Kathryn shrugged. If Gray asked her directly, she might not be able to lie, but she wasn't volunteering any information about the change in Ashley's intimate relationship with Jarrett. As she had been doing for weeks, she would encourage Gray to talk to his sister, really listen to her responses and continue offering her his unconditional support. After Kathryn had married Darren and realized it was such a terrible mistake, she might have left him sooner if she had known she had her parents' understanding.

She told Gray, "Later on tonight, maybe you should see if Ashley'll open up to you."

"She's been doing a little more of that," he admitted. "But mostly all she wants to talk about is how the bridesmaid dresses have been ordered and how she picked out a cake." He released a frustrated breath. "I'm trying, Kathryn, but it's all I can do to listen to this stuff. We should be discussing the classes she'll take in the fall."

"She is enrolled for the fall semester. You know she's already been to Lubbock a few times to look for a part-time job that will fit around her classes."

"But that doesn't really interest her," Gray said glumly. "Her head is full of romantic fluff."

"Is romance so bad?" Kathryn teased, nestling close

to his side. Resting her chin on his shoulder, she breathed in his masculine, earthy scent. "I sort of like romance myself."

"I guess it does have its good points." Gray chuckled and touched her cheek, awed as usual by the way this poised, beautiful woman could look at him as if he was something special. "Sorry to leave you in here so long, but with all the rain this week, the weeds in the garden were getting away from us."

"Tell me again what you expect to grow out there."

"Green beans, tomatoes and corn." Gray laughed at her skeptical expression. She had been needling him about this garden for weeks. "I know what I'm doing. Remember I told you I worked in the garden at my grandfather's farm every summer."

She continued to look doubtful. "That was Oklahoma. This is West Texas. Cattle and oil are the crops here."

"But that doesn't mean I can't coax a few vegetables out of the ground." He offered her his hand. "Let's go outside and I'll show you what's coming up. That is, unless you're too prissy to get into a little mud."

She stiffened, as he expected, and rose to the challenge. Kathryn hated even the hint that she couldn't get down and dirty if the need arose. She was all too aware that he had initially assessed her as a rich snob.

As he took her hand and they walked outside, he reflected, as he did frequently, on how wrong that first impression had been. Every day he discovered how warm and down-to-earth Kathryn was. She didn't seem to mind that Rick's presence cut down on their privacy. She was always pitching in—helping him paint and paper the kitchen, sharing an on-the-run meal of spaghetti and meatballs, cheering harder than anyone else at Rick's summer league baseball games. In fact, if he had to judge the past few weeks, he would put them among the best he had ever experienced. The way Kathryn was fitting into his life was surprising.

She scared him to death.

He tried to push that last thought aside, but it wouldn't go away. Since the night he and Kathryn had first made love, Gray had succeeded in "going with the flow." He had stubbornly ignored the warnings that had gone off inside him when doubts had crept in or when he began to think matters between him and Kathryn were getting too intense. He was trying to enjoy each moment as it came, without dwelling on what might happen.

"Hey, watch out!" Kathryn said, breaking into his thoughts.

Gray looked down just in time to keep from leading them both through one of the many mud puddles at the edge of his yard. "I don't see that it would matter," he said, grinning at Kathryn. "I'm already muddy enough."

"But I'm not."

"You could be," he teased.

Kathryn dropped his hand and backed away. "Oh, no, you don't."

Grinning wickedly, he moved toward her. "Come on, Kathryn. Don't you beautiful women just love mud baths?"

"Not when we're wearing brand new shorts."

"I do like that color on you," he said, sending an admiring glance up her bright blue shorts and matching blue-and-white striped top. "But the mud should wash out."

Her laughter turned to a squeal of protest as Gray

caught her around the waist and hauled her up in his arms. He held her above the muddy puddle, threatening to throw her in.

"You wouldn't."

He loosened his hold on her. She screamed and clung more tightly to him.

"I like this," he murmured, nuzzling her neck.

"You're going to drop me," she said.

Laughing, he said, "No, I'm going to kiss you."

And, as was always the case between them, a kiss that started out light and teasing quickly deepened and strengthened.

Kathryn drew back when he staggered, and accused, "You're going to drop me."

"Can I help it if you make me weak in the knees?"

"Weak? Oh, dear, and here I thought I had found a big, strong man."

With a low growl, he lowered his mouth toward hers again. "Being weak in the knees is nothing, as long as I maintain my strength in other areas."

"That's true," she murmured against his mouth. "And I have seen a few examples of your stamina."

He broke away from the kiss. "I could give you a demonstration of my strength right now. Let's go inside."

"Ashley and Rick could come back at any minute."

"We'll make it fast." His mind was already skipping ahead to thoughts of Kathryn beneath him, moving in a fast and furious rhythm, trembling with her release.

He could see from her face that her mind was moving in the same direction. Gray had turned back toward the house when a shout rang out behind them. Gray set Kathryn on her feet just as Rick, followed by his furiously yapping dogs, cleared the fence that separated the yard from the pasture. Gray and Kathryn ran to meet the red-faced, obviously agitated boy, who was covered in mud from his waist down.

"It's Sunny." Rick struggled to catch his breath. "She's stuck in some mud down by the creek. Ashley's trying to get her out, but she needs some help."

Gray took a moment to reassure Rick that this wasn't a life or death matter. Then he gathered rope from the barn, and the three of them piled onto the tractor and headed off across the pasture to the stand of trees that marked the creek's location.

Once they arrived at the site, Gray wished he had hurried. As he eased the tractor to a stop on a grassy knoll above the creek, he saw Ashley up to her waist in a pool of muddy slime, holding the white-faced, wild-eyed calf's head above the water level. Terrified for a moment, Gray jumped off and started toward her.

"Be careful!" Ashley called out. "The mud leading down here is like a water slide."

Gray paused, assessing what had happened. The week's rains had swollen the river. Part of the creek's bank had collapsed, forming a gooey cascade of mud. Today's sunshine had done little to dry out the mud, turning it instead into an oozing mess. The water Ashley and Sunny were in wasn't really even a part of the creek, just a side pool that wouldn't exist if it hadn't rained like the dickens and widened the creek.

Ashley explained that Sunny had been running from Rick, had gotten in the mud and then slid into the creek,

"Why can't she pull herself out?" Gray asked Ashley.

Ashley grimaced. "She's stuck. The mud underneath here is like glue."

"Are you stuck, too?"

"I could get out," Ashley replied. "But if I let go of Sunny, she might go under."

Rick, who remained with Kathryn near the tractor, cried out in alarm. "You've got to save her, Gray."

"We will," Gray reassured him, striding back to retrieve the rope from the tractor. He called out instructions to Ashley. "We'll try to pull you both out with just some muscle. If that doesn't work, we'll try the tractor."

"Couldn't that kind of pulling hurt Sunny?" Kathryn asked.

Gray said no, although Kathryn's worry was a consideration and the reason he wanted to try some manual pulling first. He handed one end of the rope to Kathryn and Rick, then waded gingerly down the edge of the mud slide toward Ashley and the terrified calf. The mud did remind him of rubber cement as it closed around his boots with a sucking sound. And, of course, he didn't make it down the slope upright. He fell on his rear with a splat that elicited laughter from everyone, including him, and especially from Kathryn. The only good part about the fall was that the rest of the trip down to the pool was a quick ride, ending with a splash into the muddy water beside his sister.

Unfortunately, all that activity sent Sunny into a kicking frenzy that took both Gray and Ashley to subdue. But somehow, they got the rope tied around the calf. Ashley remained with Sunny to hold her up. Gray climbed out of the muck and back onto the grassy knoll at the top of the bank in order to help Kathryn and Rick pull.

They pulled.

Sunny didn't budge.

They pulled harder.

Sunny bucked and pulled back.

Kathryn's feet flew out from under her, and she hit the mud slide bottom first. Gray imagined her terrified scream was heard some three counties over.

She slid down the bank and up to her throat in the mud before she could stop herself. And as she struggled to sit up, sputtering words he had never heard her use before, laughter sent Gray to his knees. Rick was choking with it. Ashley was laughing so hard that she couldn't keep her grip on Sunny.

Maybe the laughter was a galvanizing force. Maybe Sunny was completely disgusted with their feeble human attempts to free her. Whatever the case, she bucked so hard that she pulled herself out of the mud and clambered through the water to the bank. Before she could attempt the climb up the slippery slope, she paused near Kathryn and shook herself, slinging mud and water into Kathryn's face and hair.

"Hellfire and damnation," Kathryn screamed at the calf.

Sunny jumped backward, hooves struggling for purchase in the wet earth. Somehow, she made it up the bank, but not before her efforts sent more mud flying in Kathryn's direction. Then she trotted off, dragging the muddy rope after her.

Gray was laughing so hard he had to lie down. Rick was rolling on the ground. Ashley was whooping it up, as well. The dogs were barking. And, eventually, when Gray could finally bear to sit up and check, Kathryn began to laugh, too.

She pointed a muddy finger at him. "If I didn't know

better, I'd say you planned this whole thing, Gray Nolan."

"You just laughed a little too hard when my fanny hit the mud," he retorted.

Ashley had struggled through the pool to Kathryn's side. "Come and get us out, Gray."

"Sunny took the rope." Rick pointed in the direction his calf had taken.

Gray got to his feet, grinning down at the two women. "You guys'll just have to wait here."

Their horrified protests elicited more laughter. Without waiting for another rope, Gray managed to help them up the slope without any further disasters. Then Ashley and Rick took off across the field with the beagles, all of them chasing an unrepentant-looking Sunny.

Over her shoulder, Ashley called, "I'll get Rick cleaned up after we get this silly calf in the barn."

Kathryn raked a glob of mud from her hair and groaned. "Let's change that creature's name to Muddy."

Laughing in agreement, Gray stomped some slimy gunk off his boot.

"I've never been this dirty in my life," Kathryn said. "Even when I was a kid and used to play with the neighborhood hooligans."

"You played with hooligans?"

"I liked making my mother furious."

Laughing, he rubbed a streak of mud from her cheek. "I wonder what she'd say if she saw you like this?"

"She'd probably say I've sunk to new levels."

"I like this level," Gray murmured, dipping his head to kiss her dirty but still delectable mouth.

"I like it here, too." Kathryn smiled her pleasure. "Even wallowing in the mud is interesting with you."

Gray could feel something ease inside of him. Like ice melting beneath the warmth of Kathryn's sunny smile, a barrier deep in his soul was simply washed away. He felt...*young*. In a way he hadn't felt since he was a boy.

When his grandfather had been alive, they used to spend long afternoons in fields not so different from this one. Gray's grandfather had made a fortune investing, then retired to enjoy the good life on his farm. And because of him, Gray hadn't missed his own father too badly. His early years had been reasonably carefree, at least when his mother wasn't in love with a new man. But Ellen Nolan had been a mercurial creature, in and out of love all the time, giving Grandfather an ulcer. Each time, when the affair crumbled, she would come running home to Grandfather's farm, Gray in tow. Together, the two males would put her back together. From Grandfather, Gray learned to be a caretaker. But the older man took care of Gray, too, so he felt safe and secure. Around the time Ellen met Ashley and Rick's father, Gray's life changed profoundly. His grandfather died, the kids came along and Gray's responsibilities mounted. Eventually, he hadn't been able to see past those obligations.

But with Kathryn, Gray felt he was recapturing something free and easy within himself. With Kathryn, he felt as if he once again had someone with whom to share some burdens. Not long ago, Kathryn said he shouldn't be ashamed to need a hand now and again. He was beginning to think she was right.

He didn't want to analyze how much he was coming to depend on her. He didn't take time to pick it apart, or decide how it frightened him. Instead, he just grinned at Kathryn and nodded back toward the creek. "This could be worse, you know."

"How?"

"Well, it is June. Snakes are bad about now."

Kathryn's eyes widened. "Snakes?"

"Yep. That pool down there would be a perfect spot for a nest of water moccasins. We're lucky it wasn't."

She got on the tractor faster than Gray had believed humanly possible, her expression even more hilarious than when she'd sat in the mud. He was still laughing, and she was still fussing, plucking at her clothes as if she feared a snake might have hidden in a pocket, when they got back to the barn. They stored the tractor in the shed, then checked to see that Sunny was in her stall.

Behind the barn near Sunny's stall, before they headed to the house, Gray turned on the water hose. "We might as well get the worst of this off before we go inside." As he tugged off his socks and boots, he pointed to the water that covered the wide concrete platform under the faucet. "It looks like Ashley and Rick started their cleanup out here. At least I hope so, or I'll be cleaning dried mud out of the carpet in Rick's room for weeks."

Kathryn took off her shoes and rinsed the mud away, but she shivered when Gray turned the hose on her legs. "It's too cold."

"Not after the initial shock." To prove his point, Gray held the hose over his head, allowing the water to stream down his body. He held his finger over the end, forcing the water to spray as he worked the mud from his hair. Then he took off his filthy shirt, tossing it in a heap to the side. The water was cool, but the afternoon sun slanting from the west was warm against his skin. Closing his eyes, he let the water run over his shoulders, through the hair on his chest, across his belly, down his jean-clad legs.

When he looked up, Kathryn was leaning against the side of the barn, watching him. Her green eyes were dark, slumberous, speculative. Her gaze followed the path of the water running down his body. Her expression was one he had come to know very well this past month. An expression that made him instantly hard, reversing the natural effect of the cool water and the wet jeans he was wearing.

Grinning, he put out his hand. "Come here."

She shook her head, her voice low and sultry. "I'm too busy enjoying the view."

"I said, come here." He took hold of her hand, drawing her still-mud-caked body close. Then he lifted the hose and sent water cascading over her head.

She squealed in protest. She shivered, but she didn't move as he washed mud from her hair and her face, slaking the worst of the mess from her shorts and top and from her arms, legs and feet. He took his time about the task, enjoying touching the soft, smooth skin that emerged beneath the layer of mud. Soon he was so hot he had only one intention in mind.

As he lifted the hem of her knit blouse, Kathryn objected softly, "Gray, the kids are right inside the house."

"Probably taking a bath, getting a snack, recovering from our little adventure. They don't care what we're doing." He moved the hose so that water ran down her chest. He sighed in pleasure as her nipples became clearly outlined through her bra and the thin knit of her blouse. He slipped his hand under her blouse to cup one rounded, firm breast.

"Gray, please…" Her protest was halfhearted at best.

Taking advantage of her hesitation, Gray kissed her. The hose fell to the concrete as he backed her purposefully toward the barn wall. His hands moved expertly to the button at her waistband. The damp and still-dirty material was tough to handle, but he managed to undo the button and lower the zipper.

Kathryn pushed his hands away as he started to peel her shorts and panties down. She darted a look toward the corner of the barn. "We can't do this."

"But we can," he insisted, pushing the garments down her legs. "We'll hear the kids if they come outside. They always slam the back door."

He knelt in front of her in order to push her clothes away. He remained kneeling to kiss the nest of dark curls at the juncture of her thighs. She gasped, protesting again, but her legs parted to allow him a taste of her honeyed sweetness. She twisted under his intimate probing, gasping his name, her fingers digging into his shoulders.

Soon, groaning her pleasure, she urged him upward again. Eyes heavy with need, breath coming in short rasps, she got his jeans unbuttoned and unzipped, freeing his straining sex.

Gray bent his legs, grasped her hips and lifted her off the ground, pressing her up against the barn wall as he slipped inside her warm, velvet center. He knew the wooden wall was rough and her skin was sensitive, and he should be gentle. But there was no time for niceties, for tender words and delicate touches. Their loving was a frenzy of quick thrusts and gasping encouragements and, finally, an explosion of sensation.

For Kathryn the moment was surreal. She was aware

of fragments of her surroundings. The warming sun. The tense steel of Gray's bare, muscular shoulders beneath her hands. The taste of his kiss. The mixture of emotions inside her.

She had vowed to move in a new direction with her life. Away from the control and precision that her mother would have liked. Back toward the spontaneous, free person she had been before disappointments had forced her toward caution. Now, it would seem her journey was complete. For was there anything more wild and uninhibited than making love in the open, with discovery a very real danger? Kathryn didn't think so.

She smiled as her body relaxed against Gray's strong, solid frame. She felt such freedom, such completeness. And she couldn't imagine sharing this moment with anyone other than Gray.

She had come to need him. That emotion was much, much deeper than sexual desire, or companionship, or her wish to share in his family's closeness. She needed Gray in ways that were too important and much too confusing for her to consider right now.

Disturbed by the direction of her thoughts, she tried to move away from him. He murmured a protest and pressed her gently but firmly against the wall, continuing to support her weight with ease.

"We can't stay here like this," she told him. In answer, she felt him stir inside her once again. Stunned, she drew in a short breath. "Gray?"

"It seems I can't get enough of you."

She closed her eyes, rested her head against his shoulder and curved her legs up around his waist once again. Ripples of pleasure drifted through her as Gray continued the slow, lazy rotation of his hips.

Much as she hated the thought, she knew their love-making had to end. "They're going to send out a search party if we don't come in soon."

Gray gave a wicked little laugh and didn't stop moving.

Firmly, she said, "Gray...we didn't use...anything."

That got his attention. He drew back, severing their link. "You think there's a problem?"

"Probably not." Her period had just ended, so she felt confident she was safe.

Hugging her close again, he groaned against her neck. "I'm sorry, Kathryn. I've never gotten that carried away before."

"Me, neither," she assured him. "It's my fault as well as yours."

"It was stupid and irresponsible."

"And all the things you've prayed Ashley wouldn't be."

"Yeah." Drawing back, he looked into her eyes, the hint of a smile on his lips. "And just like all risky escapades, it was damn fun."

She agreed with a tremulous sigh. "Everything's fun with you."

He released her, letting loose with a shout of laughter.

"What's so funny?" she demanded while scrambling for her hastily discarded clothes.

Gray was rearranging his own clothing and still laughing. "No one's ever accused me of being fun."

Kathryn turned away, stepping into her wet garments, trying to make herself presentable for the kids. "So you don't sling all your girlfriends into the mud, then seduce them?"

"Only you."

She faced Gray again, a teasing retort trembling on her lips. But the words died when she caught his serious expression.

He had picked up his shirt and was shifting it from hand to hand. "There's not been anyone...like you." He opened his mouth, closed it again, adding, "No one."

The words left so much unsaid. Emotions shimmered in the air between them. Fragile and half-formed, they evaporated like morning mist. Yet the unspoken words filled Kathryn with hope. And then let her down.

Gray looked remorseful, as if he wished he hadn't spoken. His expression hardened, shutting her out. Kathryn knew she needed to say something to let him off the hook, but no words would come. Her heart was beating too loudly for her to think.

Thankfully, however, someone else was not so tongue-tied. With a loud, impatient *moo,* Sunny butted her head against the slats of her stall near the rear entrance to the barn. The sound shattered the awkwardness of the moment and gave Kathryn something other than Gray to focus on.

"You silly calf," she murmured and walked over to stroke the troublesome creature's head.

Gray watched her, saying nothing, irritated at having shattered the lightheartedness of the moment by turning serious. He didn't want to be serious, damn it. He wanted...wanted...

No, he wasn't going to think about what he wanted. Not now. Not any time soon.

Turning off the water faucet, he picked up his boots with one hand and held his other out to Kathryn.

"Come on," he said, keeping his voice and his emotions steady. "Let's go in. I've worked up an appetite."

Kathryn smiled and took his hand and tried to pretend the shifting foundation of their relationship hadn't turned into quicksand.

After that magical Sunday afternoon, Kathryn spent much of the next few weeks berating herself. June faded to July. She was with Gray just as much as before. They laughed just the same. They made love with the same sort of dizzying, intense heat she had come to expect.

But a wall had come between them.

That wall, however, didn't keep her from becoming more and more involved in his family. Her friendship with Ashley continued to deepen, and she did her best to treat the young woman like a peer. They shopped, talked about men and women, about Ashley's hopes, dreams and plans for her marriage to Jarrett and her life. Kathryn was both reassured and dismayed by their discussions. For Ashley's head was, as Gray feared, filled more with romantic schemes than with the truly practical aspects of marriage. Kathryn tried to use her own youthful marriage as an example to help Ashley, but with the folly of the young, Ashley had an answer for Kathryn's every question.

As for Kathryn's relationship with Rick, there was no word other than love to describe what had happened between them. She adored his sense of humor, tried to understand his sometimes highly emotional reactions, and did her best to accept him for the person he was. When things came to an end between Kathryn and Gray, she didn't know how Rick would react.

When they came to an end. Not if. When.

That kind of thinking tore her up. She knew she was prophesying blind, since she had no concrete proof that anything would end. Just as she had no proof that anything would endure. She didn't even know what *thing* she was worrying about. Though she knew she cared for Gray, cared deeply, she hadn't sorted through the jumble of emotions. And, of course, she had no clue to the nature of his deepest thoughts.

Several times, she started to ask Gray what he had meant when he said there had never been anyone in his life like her. In the end, however, she could never find the courage to phrase the question. She was afraid of his answer, afraid he would shrug and tell her he hadn't intended to say anything important, that his words were simply the aftermath of passion, with no deeper, stronger meaning.

And if there wasn't anything lasting brewing between the two of them, then what would come next? Would she have to walk away? Could she? Kathryn doubted she had that strength. Yet could she live from day to day in the sort of temporary arrangement they had now?

That question was gnawing at Kathryn on the mid-July day that Ashley came into the shop for the final fitting of her wedding dress. Rick and Gray were with her.

Ashley headed back to the dressing room to put on her gown with the help of Devon and the shop's alteration specialist. Rick, who was in an agreeable mood, settled down in a chair by the bay window.

Kathryn surveyed Gray with surprise. "I didn't expect to see you here today."

Gray shifted from foot to foot, nervously clearing

his throat. "This is a big deal, right? The dress has to fit perfectly before Ashley has her portrait made in it?"

"Yes."

"Then I figure if Mom were here, she wouldn't miss this."

Kathryn reached out and took his hand. "I know Ashley appreciates your being here."

He shrugged. "She acted like I'd grown two heads when I suggested it this morning."

"I'm sure she was shocked. This is like your putting your seal of approval on the wedding."

"The wedding's six weeks from Saturday." His expression was bleak. "That's not much time."

Kathryn laughed and patted his cheek. "You'll survive, Gray. And no matter what happens, I think Ashley will, too. Despite everything, she's a strong girl."

He sighed, Kathryn hugged him, and they turned together when Ashley came out of the dressing room.

If possible, she looked even more beautiful today than the first time she had tried on the gown and veil. Perhaps it was that her glorious blond hair was perfectly coiffed, and she wore the right shoes, the right undergarments and the perfect strand of pearls at her throat. But for whatever reason, she was magnificent.

Devon summed it up best. "You're a vision, Ashley."

Kathryn darted a look at Gray's face, not surprised to find him staring at his sister with undiluted awe.

Ashley stepped up on the dais in front of the mirror. "Say something," she urged her brother. "Do I look okay?"

He blinked away what looked suspiciously like tears. "You're beautiful, Ashe. So grown-up and beautiful."

Feeling moisture gathering in her own eyes, Kathryn

turned away. She was always emotional over "her" brides, but Ashley had become much more than that to her. Kathryn hoped fervently that the steps the younger woman would take down the aisle would lead her to the sort of happiness she deserved.

"Why's everybody crying?" Rick demanded. He was on his knees in the chair by the window, his arms folded across the back as he surveyed the emotional adults in the room.

Kathryn crossed to his side, wiping away her tears. "Your sister's so beautiful in her dress that we all felt like crying."

"Oh." Rick conveyed his complete disgust at their sappiness with that one short word.

Ashley, who was preening in front of the mirror, asked her younger brother, "Don't you like my dress?"

"It's okay," the boy said.

"Someday you'll understand," Gray told him.

The boy rolled his eyes and peered up at Kathryn. "What are you going to wear?"

The question was a surprise. "To Ashley and Jarrett's wedding?"

"To yours," Rick replied.

"I'm not getting married," Kathryn replied quickly. A ripple of alarm moved up her spine.

Rick looked confused. "But Gray's going to marry you. Ashley told me so."

His sister gasped. A strained silence blanketed the rest of the room.

Gazing from one adult to the other with round blue eyes, Rick said, "What's wrong?"

Though Kathryn very carefully didn't look at Gray's

face, she could hear the embarrassment in his voice as he said, "We'll talk about this later, Rick."

"But why?"

"Because I said so."

At the sternness of Gray's tone, Rick frowned. "What'd I do wrong?"

"Rick, just hush," Ashley admonished.

Kathryn found her voice at that point and told the boy, "You didn't do anything wrong."

"But we'll talk later," Gray promised him.

Devon, bless her soul, stepped forward and said breezily, "Let's get this show on the road."

"Yes, let's," Kathryn agreed, turning back to Ashley. "I think all that dress needs is a nip here and a tuck there."

Gray was silent, watching Kathryn efficiently going about her business and very carefully not looking at him.

Out of the mouths of babes, he thought, glancing at his troubled-looking brother. Strange how one young innocent's statement could stir up a hornet's nest of trouble.

Chapter Eight

"I still don't understand why everybody got mad at me."

"You just shouldn't have said anything."

Rick's and Ashley's voices caused Gray to pause in the hall outside his younger brother's bedroom. They had returned from Kathryn's shop about five-thirty, and to Gray's relief, neither Ashley nor Rick had said another word about a wedding involving Gray and Kathryn. Yet Rick had been unnaturally quiet during dinner, which signaled his little brain was churning. Gray had hoped his brother would keep quiet, so they could address this issue sometime later.

Sometime when he figured out exactly what to say.

While Gray had gone to put the beagles outside for the night, Ashley had put Rick to bed. Unlike Gray, she seemed to be having no problem talking to her younger brother about Kathryn becoming part of their family. "You don't just ask people if they're getting married," she explained as Gray hung back in the hall, listening.

"I didn't ask that," Rick protested. "I just wanted to know what kind of dress Kathryn was going to wear."

"That was the same as asking. You should have waited until they told you they were getting married before you said anything."

"But you told me they were getting married."

Gray could identify with Ashley's sigh of frustration. He often felt at a loss during discussions like this with Rick. Patiently, she said, "I told you Gray and Kathryn *might* get married. Not that they were for sure."

There was a pause before Rick said glumly, "I guess you were wrong."

"Well...maybe not."

Ashley's last statement sent Gray into action. He didn't want her filling Rick's head with still more ideas. Turning the corner into the boy's room, Gray said, "It's getting late, partner. Time for bed."

"I don't see why I have a bedtime in the summer," Rick grumbled, as he did every night.

"Because you get up early for camp." Gray picked up some of the clothes that were strewn about the room. The place was a wreck, like much of the rest of the house, evidence that lately his head hadn't been on their household, where it belonged. It was time he got his priorities back in order. He offered the garments to Ashley. "Can you put these in the hamper? And maybe help clean up around here?"

"I do my part," the young woman retorted, turning on her heel and leaving.

Very mature, Gray thought, as he tossed the clothes

onto a chair. Very adult behavior from a young woman just six weeks from her own wedding. Who would clean up after *her* when she married Jarrett?

Before he could build up a head of steam, Gray got hold of himself. Ashley was right. She did her part around here, more than her part usually, and Gray and Rick were going to have to get along without her soon enough. Gray was going to have a serious discussion about chores with his little brother. Tomorrow. Gray wasn't up for that conversation tonight. He turned toward the bed, where Rick had slipped between the covers and the cat, Bettina, had settled in a purring heap by his side. After being assured that the boy had brushed his teeth, Gray bent to tousle his hair, then started to snap off the overhead light. Rick called him back, however.

"I'm sorry," Rick said in a small voice.

Gray didn't even pretend to ask what for. Rick was upset over what he had said and the tension it had created this afternoon. "It's okay," Gray told him. "You didn't do anything wrong, and I'm sorry I acted mad at you. I'm not. But Ashley shouldn't have been talking to you about what Kathryn and I might do."

The boy's eyes brightened. "So *might* you marry her?"

Not wanting to get into a discussion, Gray said, "If I ever decide to get married, I'll tell you, okay? You won't have to hear it from Ashley."

"I wouldn't mind if you married Kathryn," Rick said, stroking his cat instead of looking at Gray. "She likes me, even more than Gina did."

Gray frowned. "Gina?" He didn't know his brother even thought about his ex-fiancée.

"I liked Gina a lot," Rick continued. "She was nice,

but Kathryn is..." He squinted up at Gray. "Kathryn's...you know." The look on his face was one of pure adoration.

"Yeah," Gray agreed reluctantly. "I know."

"So will you marry her?"

"We'll talk about this some other time." Fondly, Gray chucked Rick under the chin. "Now it's time for you to go to sleep. I hate it when you're grouchy in the mornings."

Rick seemed satisfied, but after turning out his light, Gray headed down the hall to the living room. He found Ashley sprawled on the rug, looking through a box of old photographs.

Gray wasted no time. "Don't be talking to Rick about me and Kathryn."

His sister's mouth dropped open. "Excuse me?"

"You heard me. Don't be upsetting him."

She flipped her hair off her shoulder. "I don't happen to think that answering his questions is upsetting him. He's more upset by uncertainty."

"He can come to me with his questions."

"Oh, really?" Ashley's laugh was brittle. "And what would you have said if he had asked you about marrying Kathryn?"

Frustrated because he had just ducked that very question, Gray's hands fisted at his sides.

His sister looked victorious. "I don't get you. Kathryn's terrific. You ought to be down on your knees, proposing, begging her to marry you."

"Unlike some people, I don't think marriage is something you rush into."

"And I think some people are entirely too cautious, too methodical. Marriage isn't just about practicalities. What about love?"

Yes, what about love?

That question drew Gray to the edge of a crater he didn't want to explore.

"Let's just agree to disagree," Gray said after taking a calming breath. "Except about Rick. I don't want you to tell him Kathryn and I are getting married when we're not."

She huffed in reply and turned back to the photographs.

Suddenly Gray realized what he was witnessing. His sister was home at 9:00 p.m. without Jarrett at her side. And she was doing something other than addressing wedding invitations or squealing on the telephone with one of her friends about a bridal shower or a place setting of china.

Hands on his hips, Gray said, "What are you doing here?"

She looked up in surprise. "Looking at some pictures of Mom."

"Where's Jarrett?"

Ashley's chin took on a steely edge. "He's working. As usual." The last two words dripped acid.

"Something wrong?"

"No," Ashley denied. "Jarrett's dad just hasn't been feeling too well. So Jarrett has had a lot more to do at the ranch. They're booked solid with guests for the rest of the summer."

"And Jarrett hasn't had much time for you. Or the wedding."

"We haven't been able to spend much time together," Ashley admitted. "But the wedding is all planned. Kathryn and Devon have helped me with that. Jarrett just says that whatever I want is fine with him."

The look on her face said she was none too happy about Jarrett's nonparticipation.

Much as he still didn't want this wedding to happen, Gray also didn't like seeing his sister upset. He sat down on the couch and faced her. "Come on, Ashe. I know you, so I know something's up."

She stubbornly shook her head, turning to him instead with one of the photographs she had been looking at. "This is Mom and Dad. Look how happy they seem."

Gray took the faded snapshot she offered. Their pretty mother, her blond hair a cloud around her smiling face, stood beside a tall, handsome man as fair as she. Ashley had the man's golden-hued eyes. Rick had his facial features.

And Gray hated him.

After all these years, his anger should have abated, but he couldn't stand the sight of the man who had run out on his mother, Ashley and Rick. Run out and left Gray to shoulder his burdens. And in Gray's book, there was nothing more dishonorable than deserting your family.

"Did you ever like him?" Ashley's quiet question revealed that Gray was doing a poor job of hiding his feelings. Which was bad. One of the few promises his mother had elicited from him before she died was that he wouldn't fill the kids' heads with too much poison about their father.

Careful to keep his tone calm, Gray answered Ashley's question. "He was all right at first."

"Then they were happy for a little while?"

The wistfulness of the question touched Gray. "Sure they were happy," he said, trying to dig up memories he had buried along with his childhood. "They loved

music. The Eagles. The Rolling Stones. Don't you remember how they used to play it loud and dance
around the kitchen, cooking, drinking wine.'' He
laughed softly, thinking of how his mother used to try
to get him to join them. ''They embarrassed the hell
out of me in front of my friends. Parents weren't supposed to act like that.''

Looking sad, Ashley sighed. ''I don't remember
them that way. I just remember the fights.''

Gray sat forward, hands clasped between his knees,
wishing he could erase her bitter memories, but knowing from personal experience that he couldn't.

Ashley picked up another photograph, one of their
mother with Gray when he was very small. ''She was
so young when she had you.''

Something in her expression touched off an alarm
inside Gray. ''Ashley, what's all this about?''

''I'm just looking at pictures,'' she said, a crease of
irritation forming between her eyebrows. ''Why are
you so suspicious?''

''You're just in a strange mood, and Jarrett hasn't
been around here much. I'm thinking there's some
problem.''

Ashley exhaled and darted him an irritated glance.
''You always think there's a problem.''

''I'm usually right when it comes to our family.''

She shrugged off his gloomy comment and plucked
still another photo from the box beside her. ''Rick
looks a lot like Dad,'' she murmured.

''Something the bastard didn't wait around to discover.''

Ashley bit her lip. ''Gray, do you think Mom got
pregnant with Rick because she thought Dad would
stay if they had another baby?''

That was exactly what Gray had always thought, though he had never said the words aloud. He was a bit surprised to see that Ashley had figured it out. "Why she got pregnant doesn't matter," he told his sister. "She wanted Rick so much. She almost died having him, and she got really sick afterward, but she was crazy about Rick."

Even now, Gray could remember his mother's joy at having her youngest child. She had been forty-two, her husband was gone and the pregnancy had been high-risk. Yet she had forged ahead with the same spirit that had always carried her. His mother, impetuous and romantic, always thought she could do anything. Money hadn't been a big problem, since she had a decent job as well as money from Grandfather's estate and the sale of his farm.

When his mother had Rick, Gray had been working his way through his last year of college. Though he hadn't lived at home since high school, he had remained close to his mother and to Ashley. He had been happy when his stepfather packed his things and disappeared. Maybe it had been that attitude that kept his mother from telling him she was pregnant until she couldn't hide her condition. Gray remembered he'd been seeing a girl, sleeping with her mainly, who had thought it was so cool that his mother was pregnant. Gray hadn't thought it cool. He had been horrified.

And later, when his mother's cancer was diagnosed and she was dying, he had silently cursed her folly at bringing Rick into the world. Losing her and dealing with Ashley's grief was bad enough. Rick's needs had made the situation almost impossible. There had been times in that first year after his mother's death that Gray had wished Rick had never been born.

Now he couldn't imagine his world without his temperamental little brother. But in the beginning he had been unprepared for the responsibility. He had been in school, busy dealing with the practicalities of life. Rick had been shuttled from one sitter to the next, one friend after another. By the time Gray got a handle on the scope of raising a child, some damage had been done. Gray spent the years since trying to make up for his initial mistakes.

Gray summoned a smile for Ashley and repeated, "It doesn't really matter why Mom had Rick. He's here. We're not sending him back."

She grinned, though her expression sobered. "But it was kind of desperate, wasn't it? Her getting pregnant that way when everything was falling apart?"

Gray studied his sister in silence for a moment before the question pressing on his mind popped out. "Are you worried that you're pregnant, Ashe?"

She dropped the photo. "What?"

"You're making me crazy with all this talk about Mom being young when she had me and then having Rick to hang on to your dad." He paused to peer even more sharply at her. "You're not thinking of trapping Jarrett with a baby, are you?"

"Trapping him?" Ashley repeated, horrified.

"Is he backing out of the wedding?" Gray demanded.

"Of course not!"

"Then why the hell haven't I seen him lately?"

"Jeez, a few months ago, you told him to get out and stay out. Now you're worried because he's not around." Ashley tossed the picture she held into the box and reached for the lid. "I can't believe you'd think I would do something as stupid as getting pregnant.''

"It's been known to happen.''

She got to her feet, her face scarlet with rage. "Did Kathryn tell you she was worried about me getting pregnant?''

"Why would she do that?''

"Ever since she found out Jarrett and I are sleeping together—''

"What?'' Gray interrupted, puzzled. "When did you start sleeping with him?''

Tawny eyes blazing, Ashley said, "That's none of your business.''

"Ashley—''

"It was probably about the same time you started sleeping with Kathryn.''

He drew in a deep breath, trying to remain calm. His head was buzzing with all the information his sister had revealed. "You're sure you're not pregnant?''

"I already said I wasn't. What do you want, a test?''

"No,'' Gray said, getting to his feet. He put his hands on Ashley's shoulders, looking her straight in the eye. He needed to keep his cool, not go nuts about this. "Something's wrong between you and Jarrett. Something that has you very upset. Can't you tell me?''

She looked away, though Gray could see the tears that tipped her long, dark lashes. "Everything's different than I expected,'' she admitted at last. "Ever since me and Jarrett...'' Her gaze skittered toward Gray and then away again. "Since we went...ahead...well, he's different. He works all the time. We don't go out. He's saving money, he says, for our future. But he doesn't seem very excited about making plans. And when we're together, all he wants to do is..."

Her expression was pure misery as she looked up at Gray again. "He's just different. Everything's turning out different than I planned."

Gray swallowed hard, wishing with all his heart he could erase the confusion and disillusionment from her features. As he had suspected all along, his sister wasn't ready for the responsibilities of an adult relationship. In terms of years, she was all grown up. But in some respects, she was still an uncertain young girl. He might get his wish; this wedding might not happen. But he had never wanted Ashley to be suffering as she was now.

"You could put off the wedding," Gray told her. When she began a protest, he held up a hand to stop her. "I didn't say end the engagement. I said postpone it. You could take some time to think this through."

"All the plans have been made."

"They can be changed."

Sighing, Ashley rubbed her forehead. "I love him, Gray."

For the first time, he actually believed those words. But he held tight to the belief he had always held. "Marriage takes more than love," he said.

She was silent for a moment, staring glumly at the floor.

Gray slipped a hand under her chin and lifted her face so that he could look her in the eye. "It's all right to be confused, you know. Love and sex and all that stuff are pretty complicated."

"For you, too?"

He wasn't expecting the conversation to shift to him.

"Are you confused about how you feel about Kathryn?" Ashley prodded him.

"We're not talking about me."

"I wish you wouldn't brush me off like that. If you can talk to me about my love life, why can't I talk to you about yours?"

It was a good question, to which he had only one answer. "I guess I'm so confused that I don't know what to say about Kathryn."

"But you two are so right together."

If they were so right, Gray had to wonder why Kathryn hadn't bothered to tell him about the serious change in Ashley and Jarrett's relationship. That felt like a betrayal of trust to him.

Grimly, he said, "Whether we're right for each other or not remains to be seen. It's not something you should worry about."

"But Gray—"

He interrupted her with a brotherly hug. "I don't want to talk about this now. You look tired, kiddo. You ought to go to bed and try to get some rest. It seems to me you've got some serious thinking to do in the next couple of days."

Ashley agreed, but before she reached the hall, Gray said, "Will you check in on Rick?"

"How come?"

"I think I'm going to go talk to Kathryn."

His sister looked alarmed. "You're mad at her for not telling you about me and Jarrett."

"I just want to talk," Gray replied evasively. "Maybe clear up some of the confusion I'm feeling."

With a reluctant nod, Ashley went toward Rick's room.

Gray went out into the hot Texas night. The weather suited his mood. For he was mad as fire at Kathryn.

"Thank goodness that's the last batch." Devon stooped to pull a tray of miniature quiches from the oven.

"Just in time for me to collapse." On the other side of the kitchen, Kathryn raked a forearm across her perspiring face. She and Devon had been working since the shop closed, preparing food for an engagement party to be held tomorrow evening. Normally, they might not have taken on such a big, last-minute job on a weekend when they already had two weddings scheduled. But the party was for a prominent local businessman's daughter and her fiancé, and it could turn into more business in the long run.

"You look beat." Devon joined Kathryn at the counter where she was wrapping ham slices around melon wedges.

"It's so hot. I just hope this melon stays crisp until tomorrow night. Maybe we should have waited."

"We have no time to do this tomorrow," Devon reminded her. "It'll be fine in the refrigerator."

Stifling a groan, Kathryn stretched and rubbed at the ache in her lower back.

"You okay?" Devon asked. "You've been rubbing your back like that all day."

Grimacing, Kathryn said, "It's that time of the month. My back always kills me just before I get my period."

"And you're also upset about what happened with Gray this afternoon."

Kathryn pretended not to hear her friend's comment,

but that was a difficult stance to maintain since Devon was right by her side.

"I've never seen two people freak out so completely over a kid's innocent question."

"We didn't freak out."

"You froze, and Gray looked like a grizzly bear staring down the barrel of a gun."

After placing the last slice of melon in the plastic storage container in front of her, Kathryn turned to the other woman with an exasperated sigh. "I don't feel like getting into this, Devon."

"I'm sorry." The other woman's brown eyes grew wide with concern. "I didn't mean to upset you more."

Suddenly contrite, Kathryn slipped her arm through her friend's. "I'm the one who's sorry. And sometime when I'm not dead on my feet, and my back's not killing me, I might have a discussion with you about Gray. Frankly, I could probably use your advice."

Devon laughed. "I don't know, Kathryn. I've been thinking lately that I ought to get out of the romantic-advice business. After all, I can't run my own love life."

Since Devon had never before mentioned that she had a love life, Kathryn was surprised. "Maybe what we both need is some therapy. I think I'll check our group insurance policy to see what's covered."

"Sounds good," Devon agreed with a laugh.

The two of them worked in companionable silence for a few minutes, loading the dishwasher and storing the last of the food in the refrigerator. By the time they were finished, the ache in Kathryn's lower back was intense.

Devon picked up her purse and started toward the

door. Kathryn followed, eager to lock up and get upstairs to bed.

But before she left, Devon turned back to Kathryn. "I just want to say one thing to you about Gray."

"Devon, please—"

"If you love him, tell him."

Kathryn sighed.

"You do love him, don't you?"

There seemed little point in lying. To Devon or to herself. "Yes, I do love him," Kathryn told her friend. "And it's not what I set out to do."

Devon chuckled. "Since when do any of us plan on falling in love?"

"But Gray's a mess," Kathryn said. "His hands are full with his practice and dealing with Rick's emotional problems and Ashley's romantic escapades. He doesn't want a relationship any more than I do. We're not that serious."

"Then why are you together almost every day?"

Kathryn shrugged. She didn't want to face the dichotomies in her relationship with Gray. "He can't even express any of his feelings for me, except maybe in bed."

Arching one eyebrow in interest, Devon said, "But the communication there is pretty good, right?"

Kathryn's cheeks betrayed her by burning, but she ignored Devon's chuckle as she continued, "Maybe Gray is right to hesitate. When I think back to just two months ago, to the life I worked so hard to keep simple and easy—"

"And boring," Devon put in. "And terribly celibate."

"Terribly," Kathryn agreed with a sigh.

"You need to tell him how you feel." Her expression serious, Devon touched Kathryn's arm. "Take it from me, you might regret not telling him. Something could happen, then you would feel..." She paused, chewing on her bottom lip. "You'd be sorry, Kathryn. I know because I...well..."

Kathryn relieved Devon's reluctant soul-baring before it could continue. "There's someone you wish you had told that you loved."

Devon nodded. The naked pain in her eyes confirmed Kathryn's longtime suspicion that Devon had some secret that kept her from pursuing the romance she promoted so avidly with others.

"Maybe it's not too late to tell this guy that you love him," Kathryn suggested softly.

"Yes, it is." Her voice held the sort of finality that brooked no further conversation. Instead, she gave Kathryn a hug and opened the back door to leave. Gray was standing on the porch. Devon jumped, then pressed a hand to her chest. "My God, Gray, you scared me to death. Why didn't you knock on the door?"

He muttered an apology to Devon, though his gaze was on Kathryn. "We need to talk. *Now.*"

An intense discussion with Gray was the last thing Kathryn wanted, but his tone wasn't one that invited a protest. Kathryn caught the questioning look Devon sent her way, but waved her friend off. "See you tomorrow."

Devon exited, leaving Kathryn to face Gray. A very upset Gray, she realized, taking in his squared jaw and clenched fists as he came into the kitchen.

Her pulse quickening, she stepped forward. "What's wrong? Is it Rick? Ashley?"

"Apparently I was wrong to trust you." Gray bit the words out with ugly precision.

"What does that mean?"

"You know Ashley and Jarrett are sleeping to-gether."

She bit her lip. "Yes."

"And you didn't tell me."

"She asked me not to."

"So what!" Cursing, he slapped a fist into his palm. "For God's sake, Kathryn, you know how I've felt about this whole relationship she's had with Jarrett. Up until now, the one bright spot turned out to be that she hadn't slept with him yet. Without that deep an in-volvement, I felt like there was hope that she'd pull away."

Kathryn gaped at him in surprise. "But you told me you suggested she sleep with him, hoping it was just a case of lust."

"That was stupid of me." His forehead creased with new worry. "Now she's slept with him, and there's a whole new—"

"Oh, just stop it," Kathryn told him sharply. "Stop going on like this is some horrible tragedy. They're young and healthy and in love. Their making love is natural and probably inevitable. Ashley has assured me several times that they never take chances. She's not stupid. And Jarrett's very responsible."

"Even the most responsible people can get carried away."

We have.

The words burned into Kathryn's brain as she re-membered their wild and unprotected Sunday-afternoon lovemaking behind his barn. But her mo-mentary fear was quieted as her lower back throbbed, a tangible reminder that there should be no pregnancy as the result of their foolishness nearly three weeks ago.

Gray's expression grew even more thunderous. "Did you tell Ashley that it was fine and natural and inevitable that she was sleeping with Jarrett?"

"No, but I tried not to sit in judgment of her, either. I decided that was just a little too hypocritical."

"You should have told me," Gray growled.

"What would you have done?" she retorted. "You had already done everything you could think of to break them up. I doubt anything you could have done or said would have had a major impact on this situation."

"You don't know that. And now Ashley's all confused. It seems that ever since Mr. Perfection Jarrett McMullen got what he wanted, things have changed. Even the wedding may be off."

"Then you must be happy," Kathryn snapped.

"You'd think so, wouldn't you?" He pushed a frustrated hand through his hair. "But Ashley's hurt and scared. I think she's afraid Jarrett's just been using her."

"I don't believe for one minute that Jarrett is that sort of young man. There's more between those two than sex. But like all men, he's probably completely unable to express his feelings." Kathryn meant the last statement for Gray's benefit, but he was so caught up in his rage over Kathryn's supposed interference with Ashley that he ignored the gibe.

"I might have been able to talk to Ashley about this before tonight if I'd had all the facts," Gray said, harsh accusation in his face. "If you had told me—"

"Oh, give it up," Kathryn retorted. "You know damned well that Ashley wasn't going to talk to you about anything important until she was good and ready."

"But she talked to you about this."

"She didn't come to me and have a long conversation about it. It slipped out one day when we were talking."

"You should have told me. She's my sister, not yours."

Kathryn was silent a moment, struggling to control her anger. "But I care about her, too. I'd have told you if I thought she was in serious danger."

"But you're not part of our family. You don't have the right to make decisions about her, or about anything to do with us."

The cold words took Kathryn's breath. She tried not to betray her emotions, but they welled up inside. She turned and walked quickly across the kitchen, hoping to hide her distress from Gray. But she wasn't fast enough.

She felt him come up behind her. He placed a gentle hand on her shoulder. "I'm sorry, Kathryn. I didn't mean to hurt you."

She waited, thinking he would take back his brutal statement about her rights where his family was concerned. She wanted him to reassure her that she was, indeed, an important part of his life, that she had a right to care about his sister, his brother, about him. She needed him to say he cared for her. He might think his feelings could be expressed by his touch; his passion might be in the fire they built when they made love, but she wanted more than that.

Gray, however, said nothing else. And that silence told her exactly what sort of place she occupied in his life. Maybe that was what she deserved. A woman who had virtually no relationship with her own family wasn't qualified to interfere in his.

Without turning, she said, "I think you should go."

He didn't move. "I didn't mean to be so harsh, Kathryn."

"Oh, I think you did exactly what you meant to do."

Grasping her upper arm, he forced her to face him. "I'm upset about Ashley, Kathryn. She's confused and afraid and hurting. Some of that might have been avoided if you had told me what she was getting into. Maybe I could have helped her."

Kathryn started to protest again, then reconsidered. He wasn't about to listen to anything she said. He was stubborn, opinionated and all-knowing. He was just one more man who thought he could control the world of those around him. And she should have known better than to get involved with him in the first place.

"Weren't you leaving?" she said as coldly as she could.

Gray's troubled blue eyes searched her face. "Don't you understand why I'm upset?"

Rage boiled up inside her. "Of course I understand. You're the one who doesn't have a clue. As usual."

"What the hell does that mean?"

"You're not angry about Ashley. You're furious over this afternoon, about what Rick said and the awkwardness it caused."

He fell back a step, his face hardening. "Rick's just a kid. He didn't mean anything."

"But he scared you to death."

"Don't be ridiculous." Gray turned toward the door. "You're angry and tired. We'll talk about this some other time."

"No, we won't," she said just before he reached the door. "We won't talk about this again because you don't want to talk about it. You're going to stay angry.

You'll simmer about this. You'll convince yourself that you're angry about my not telling you about Ashley and Jarrett. You'll decide you can't trust me, and you'll pull away. But that's not what the problem is." She drew in a deep breath. "You're angry because you've allowed yourself to care for me."

His broad shoulders twitched as though she had touched him, but he didn't turn around.

She forced herself to continue. "You're angry because I care for you."

His hand reached for the doorknob.

And she went for broke. "You're angry because I love you."

He hesitated. For half a second, his clean, handsome profile was silhouetted against the light burning on the back porch. But he didn't look at her before he left.

To the door that closed behind him, Kathryn whispered, "Coward."

The tears that had gathered in her eyes dried up. A long time ago, Kathryn Seeger had promised herself she would never cry over another man. She'd be damned if she would break that vow tonight.

The tears came nearly two weeks later.

By then, Kathryn knew Gray wasn't going to call her. She hadn't seen him or Rick since the day Ashley tried on her gown. Even Ashley was curiously absent, not even picking up the dress that was now perfectly altered and was hanging, pristine and beautiful, in one corner of Kathryn's office. The hole Gray's absence left in Kathryn's life was big enough to swallow the whole state of Texas. When she stretched it to include Ashley and Rick, the borders expanded even farther.

But that aching crater of loneliness was nothing

compared to Kathryn's growing suspicion that she was pregnant.

Yes, *pregnant*.

Many days passed before Kathryn worked up the courage to confront that possibility. The backache she'd had the last night she saw Gray had not resulted in a period; no period was in sight, and she was now two full weeks late. It had been over five weeks since the Sunday afternoon in June when she and Gray had made love without protection. She had to face facts. There was every reason in the world to think she was pregnant.

Pregnant. With Gray's child.

One evening, Kathryn stopped running from that possibility and went out to buy pregnancy tests. Two of them. She was going to try one that night, because she couldn't wait. She'd save the other one for tomorrow, because she knew an early-morning test was supposedly the most reliable.

A baby. God, what had they done?

Standing in the checkout line at the drugstore, Kathryn thought of the television commercials for the home pregnancy tests. The ads always showed a happy, but anxious couple, waiting together for the results. But the first time Kathryn had used one of these, she had been alone. She had been too afraid to tell her ex-husband she might be pregnant. And now, here she was again, all by herself. Paying for the tests, Kathryn avoided the clerk's eyes, afraid she would cry if anyone even looked at her with interest or sympathy.

Inside her were tightly strung emotions. Fear. Anger. Joy. Yes, strangely enough, she felt something akin to excitement. After the loss of her first baby and the dissolution of her marriage, Kathryn had told herself not to think about children ever again. But growing deep in her womb right now might be a baby. Gray's baby. Though Kathryn was levelheaded enough to see the problems that lay ahead, she would never see this child as anything but a precious gift.

Kathryn hurried home from the drugstore, eager to find out the truth. But before she could break open the test package, Ashley arrived at Kathryn's apartment door. Ashley, who looked young and vulnerable, tearfully said she needed to talk. Kathryn didn't have the heart to turn her away.

Ashley was considering calling off the wedding. Kathryn was feeling none too qualified to address anyone else's problems and could barely follow what the young woman was saying. The gist of it was that Jarrett had no time for Ashley these days. He was worried about his father's health and the family ranch's finances, but wouldn't open up to Ashley about either issue. Worst of all, he now expressed little excitement about the wedding. He wouldn't call it off, however, leaving that ball firmly in Ashley's court.

Ashley said the only intimacy they shared these days was making love. Jarrett made her feel as if that was all he wanted from her. Sex, which she had always imagined would draw her and Jarrett closer, had muddied the issues between them instead. She was seriously considering canceling the wedding, but her fear was that, in doing so, she would lose Jarrett completely. She had come to Kathryn because Gray had been so against the wedding in the first place that Ashley wasn't sure she could depend on his advice.

And all Kathryn could do was tell Ashley to follow her heart. It was lame advice, and Kathryn knew it, but she couldn't think of what else to say.

"Are you and Gray following your hearts?" Ashley

asked, her tone sarcastic as she pulled herself out of her chair. "Is that why you're apart?"

Kathryn, who remained on the sofa, didn't reply.

Ashley released a glum sigh. "I feel like this fight you guys had is all my fault. I know Gray was furious with you for not telling him about me and Jarrett sleeping together."

"We fought about much more than that," Kathryn assured her. "So don't worry. In a way, my problem with your brother is a lot like your problem with Jarrett. No communication."

The younger woman chewed on her bottom lip for a moment. "Rick misses you a lot, you know."

"I miss him, too." Guilt stabbed through Kathryn. She was sure her sudden absence was upsetting to Rick and fed his emotional insecurities. But what was she supposed to do? Gray had made it clear she was not an important part of his life, nor the lives of his siblings. That knowledge continued to sting like iodine on a fresh wound. Feeling the pain keenly, Kathryn stood and took Ashley's hand. "I miss all of you so very much."

"Then call Gray."

She might have a real reason to call him. A reason he wouldn't like.

"He's miserable."

Kathryn felt a flicker of hope. "Is he?"

"He's gone on this incredible home-improvement frenzy. All the jobs he'd been saving up for months are getting done. The house has never looked better."

"It doesn't sound like he's suffering too much."

"Sure he is. Constant activity is how Gray deals with any emotional upheaval."

"Because if he's busy enough he might not have to deal with his emotions at all," Kathryn murmured.

Ashley sent Kathryn a long, considering glance. "You really do understand him, don't you?"

With a bitter laugh, Kathryn shook her head. "I'm wondering if men and women ever really understand one another."

Concern flickered across Ashley's features. "Are you okay? You seem really down, depressed."

"Like I said, I miss you guys."

"But you're so pale."

"I'm just tired," Kathryn assured her. "Don't worry about me. Concentrate on yourself and what you want to do. You've got to give this wedding some long and careful thought. Somehow, you've got to get Jarrett to talk to you."

"Even if I don't know what I want to do?"

"A really good, truthful conversation with him could clear things up."

"I could give you the same advice." Ashley gave her a sudden, hard hug. "Oh, Kathryn. Gray's a fool if he lets you go. We all need you so much. Please talk to him, soon. Promise?"

The entreaty was more than Kathryn could withstand. Ashley wouldn't leave or let Kathryn off the hook until she had elicited a promise that she would talk to Gray. Knowing she was about to dissolve, Kathryn promised and sent the younger woman off with a hug and a message of love to Rick. She vowed that she would see the little boy, no matter what was happening with her and Gray.

Ashley gone, Kathryn faced the test in the bathroom. She tried it again in the morning.

Both times, the result was the same.

And that's when she cried.

Chapter Nine

As Gray seated himself across the kitchen table from Ashley and Jarrett, he saw that his sister's fiancé had changed. The rancher's son was leaner, more manly; his sun-bronzed face had lost its youthful roundness. Maybe the differences were more noticeable because Gray had tried so hard not to pay attention to Jarrett this summer. But in Gray's estimation, these past two months had left a mark of maturity on Jarrett Mc-Mullen.

The changes made it easier for Gray to begin what he was afraid would be a difficult conversation. "I'm glad you two said you'd sit down for a talk. Rick is spending the night at Tommy's, so I thought this would be a good time for some decisions to be made about the wedding."

Jarrett returned Gray's regard with a steady gaze. Ashley looked at her hands.

Gray was perplexed that his sister wasn't her usual firebrand self, but that was why he had asked the kids to talk to him tonight. Because Ashley was a mess. She moped about the house, vacillating between tears and anger. She had made no decision about the wedding, which was now about three weeks away. It seemed to Gray that a decision needed to be reached. If no wedding was taking place, plans should be unmade. They would need to notify Kathryn...

At the thought of her, Gray's focus shattered. He hadn't seen her in nineteen days. Nineteen long, hard days. He had tried filling them up as best he could, but there were still times like this when all he could do was see Kathryn's face, smell her scent, feel her in his arms, hear her soft voice telling him she loved him.

"Gray?"

He looked up from his Kathryn-induced haze to find Ashley and Jarrett eyeing him with curiosity. He shook his head to clear his thoughts. "I'm sorry, I zoned there for a minute."

"You do that a lot lately," Ashley said dryly.

"So do you," Gray shot back. "That's what I want to talk about." Jarrett heaved a sigh, and Gray shifted his attention to him. "What do you think? Is this wedding still on?"

The younger man blinked, no doubt caught off guard by the directness of the question. His expression hardened. "Look, Gray, this is between me and Ashley."

"So you've made a decision?"

Jarrett's gaze fell. Ashley was curiously silent.

"Hey, guys," Gray said, leaning forward. "I know you think all I've done is butt in to your affairs, but it looks to me like I have to. Over the past couple of weeks, everything about this wedding has ground to a halt. And no matter how pleased I might be if you decide to wait—''

"Yeah, I'm sure you'd like that," Jarrett said sarcastically.

Gray ignored him. "There are some matters that have to be attended to if the wedding's off." He looked at his sister's bowed head. "The answering machine is full of calls from Devon about the food for the reception. She needs some decisions. And in just three days, your friends are going to a lot of trouble and expense to throw a barbecue and shower in your honor."

He shifted his attention back to Jarrett. "And isn't your aunt giving a party for you guys the weekend after that? I bet she's getting the invitations ready, preparing food, all that sort of thing. Is it fair to let these people go on assuming there's going to be a wedding if there's not?"

The young man said nothing to Gray, but darted a miserable look at Ashley, who didn't look at him or move.

Gray threw up his hands. "If you aren't going to get married—"

"We haven't said that," Jarrett put in, his dark eyes glittering with resentment.

Sending the young man a hard look of his own, Gray demanded, "So you are definitely planning to marry my sister in three weeks?"

Jarrett opened his mouth, but no sound came out.

"Let me warn you about one thing." Narrowing his eyes, Gray leaned across the table to get right in the younger man's face. "I can tell you this. You're not pulling any immature, cowardly stunts like leaving her standing at the altar."

Ashley inhaled sharply, but still didn't look up from her hands, which were now clenched.

Jarrett glared at Gray, his neck turning a dull red. "I'm not a coward. I'm not immature. You've said that all along, without bothering to get to know me at all."

The words were an echo of some of Kathryn's observations. Gray admitted their truth. "You're right, Jarrett. I don't know you that well. I apologize."

The young man grunted a reply.

"What do you think about this?" Gray demanded of his sister.

She finally looked up. Her tawny eyes were swimming with tears. "I don't know."

"Shouldn't you make a decision?" Gray tried to keep his tone gentle, sensing Ashley was near the breaking point, but feeling she had to face the inevitable.

She dashed a hand across her eyes, then looked at Jarrett, whose head was now bowed. Her face crumpled. "Then it's off, I guess."

Surprised, Gray bit his lip. Jarrett sat as if turned to stone.

With jerky movements, Ashley stood, sending her chair banging to the floor. Her voice was choked. "I'm so glad both of you have gotten what you wanted from me."

She ran from the kitchen. A door slammed down the hall. Both men winced.

After several long, uncomfortable moments, Jarrett broke the silence. "Are you going to talk to her?"

Gray regarded the young man with cold disdain. "Seems to me you're the one who has some explaining to do to her."

"You're the one who forced this issue," Jarrett retorted.

Gray got up from the table. "Don't lay this on me. You know as well as I do that a decision had to be faced about this, and you two weren't doing it on your own."

"But 'big brother' can always be counted on to make sure we do the right thing." The jeering note in Jarrett's voice was punctuated by the way he slung himself out of his chair and stomped toward the door.

Gray knew he should let him go. If Jarrett left now, without discussing this further with Ashley, her heart would be broken. The romance would be over for good. Gray should have been pleased by that prospect. But somehow, he just couldn't do that to his little sister. He knew how a heart could ache. His was throbbing right now.

So, in a voice that dripped sarcasm, Gray called out to Jarrett before he could leave. "That's right. Just let Ashley alone. Let her cry. That'll prove to her you only cared about one thing."

Jarrett pivoted to face Gray again. "What do you mean?"

"Don't you get it? She thinks all you wanted was to sleep with her."

"That's crap!" Jarrett shouted. "Ashley knows I love her. I could sleep with a dozen girls, but I wanted to marry her."

"Wanted?" Gray repeated. "That's past tense." To make a point, he was deliberately cruel. "What changed? Did you reconsider once the chase was over, once you'd had her?"

With just two long strides, Jarrett crossed the kitchen to stand nearly nose to nose with Gray. Voice tight, fists curled, he said, "You make one more crack like that, and I'll hit you. You don't talk about her like that, do you hear me? It wasn't like that with me and her, and you can't talk about her that way. Nobody can. You do it again, and I'll kill you."

Merely lifting an eyebrow at the young man's threats, Gray said softly, "If you feel this strongly about my sister, shouldn't you be talking to her?"

Jarrett rocked backward as if struck. He wavered there, eyes fastened on Gray. Then he turned and stalked down the hall. A moment later, Gray heard him pounding on Ashley's bedroom door, calling her name. To her credit, she made him beg. Gray listened to their tearful, shouted exchange, half of him hoping she would send Jarrett on his way. And yet he smiled when she finally let Jarrett in.

"That was very slick."

Kathryn's soft comment jerked Gray around. She stood in the doorway of the utility porch. And the sight of her—after nineteen days without her—simply took his breath away. Had she always been this beautiful? Her hair this glossy black? Her eyes so misty green? And had any other woman ever looked as good as she did in a short tan skirt and white sleeveless blouse?

Realizing he was beginning to zone out once again, Gray tried to steel himself against Kathryn's special appeal. "What are you doing here?"

She flinched at his tone. "I'm sorry. I shouldn't have just walked in. I guess I'm just used..." Her voice faltered, then she lifted her chin. "I always came in this way before, but I shouldn't have this time."

Gray resisted the urge to tell her it was okay, that she could come in his house any way she wanted. But he couldn't say something like that, not when he had to stay away from her. For her sake and his, they didn't need to be together.

"Why'd you do that just now with Jarrett?" she asked.

"Do what?"

"You sent him back to Ashley when he could have just as easily left."

"Sounds like you were eavesdropping as well as walking in uninvited."

"I heard enough to be surprised," Kathryn retorted. "Why didn't you just let Jarrett go?"

Gray turned to the kitchen sink, where dishes from the morning were still piled. He needed to get busy, so busy he didn't have to look at Kathryn. "Not that it's any of your business, but they're calling off the wedding. I think it'll be better if they talk it out instead of staying angry."

Bitterness laced Kathryn's laughter. "Imagine that. Gray Nolan advises someone to talk something out."

Stubbornly, Gray ran water in the sink. "You and I don't have anything to talk out."

There was silence. Then a soft, "Oh, but we do."

He turned around, accepting that his forced coldness wasn't going to scare her off. He resorted to a much more brutal approach. "I don't love you, Kathryn."

She didn't even blink. "I know that."

"Then what is there to talk about?"

Pushing a nervous hand through her hair, she said, "There's something you need to know."

He exhaled, briefly closed his eyes, then took a step toward her. "Let's not do this, okay? We could hash this thing over and over again. We can look at it from all sides. But we're still going to be left with the same conclusion. You want something from me that I can't give. I don't want to marry you."

"I never asked you to."

"And I'm not much of a believer in love."

"That's not true."

He brushed her protest aside with a sweep of his arm. "It is true. And besides, I've known from the minute I met you that we're not suited to one another."

Kathryn made a disgusted sound. "Are you still singing that sad, old tune?"

Gray ignored her. "From the minute we met, I was attracted to you. I couldn't get you out of my mind. But I also knew there was no way a fancy boutique owner, someone as sophisticated and polished and perfect as you, was going to fit into my life."

"That's a silly excuse," she said. "I know because I tried using it myself. It didn't work. I still fell in love with you."

"Don't get me wrong. You're a wonderful person. Easy to talk to. Fun to be with." His voice deepened. "A wonderful lover."

Kathryn's gaze faltered under his regard. She turned away, lifting a shaky hand to her forehead.

Gray took a step toward her, wishing he could massage the ache from her head. Instead, he kept his hands balled at his sides. "You've been wonderful to Rick and Ashley. They love you."

Voice trembling, but shoulders straight, Kathryn said, "Ashley said Rick misses me."

Miss was too mild a word for the withdrawal Rick was having from Kathryn. Gray hated that most of all, but he knew it would pass. This was for the best in the long run. "I shouldn't have let him get so close to you."

"Oh, yes," Kathryn muttered, looking him straight in the eye again. "Just as you shouldn't have *let* me love him. Or love you."

Gray swallowed. "Kathryn, please—"

"Just shut up, okay?" Her voice was steady now, as firm as her gaze. "If you can stop trying to control this situation for just one second, I've got something to say to you."

"I don't want to fight—"

"Neither do I. I want you to stand there and listen. Don't try to interrupt. You aren't the boss right now. Much as I know you love to control everything."

He frowned. "Come on, Kathryn. I know you're angry and hurt—"

"I'm pregnant."

"But that's no reason to..." His voice clogged in his throat as the words sank in.

"Pregnant," Kathryn repeated. She kept her chin up, as if daring him to ask her for clarification.

"You can't..." No sooner was the denial out of his mouth than Gray remembered that Sunday afternoon out by the barn. Kathryn covered in mud, watching him wash himself with the hose. He remembered undressing her, taking her, up against the barn wall. He had taken her with no thought for the consequences, and now she was pregnant.

Thrusting fingers through his hair, he stood, reeling from the shock, sputtering, "You said you were safe."

She gave a harsh little laugh. "I guess what they taught us in health class in junior high is the truth— there really aren't any safe days."

Swallowing hard, Gray stared at her, his gaze drawn to the flat stomach beneath her trim skirt. "You're sure about this?"

"I did a test myself last Friday and saw my doctor this morning. It's early, but I'm definitely pregnant."

"Last Friday?" he repeated. She had lived with this knowledge for nearly six whole days without telling him. Maybe that was why she was so calm. She'd had all this time to get used to the situation.

Situation? It's a baby, not a situation.

"So..." She released the word like a long-held breath. "I just wanted you to know."

With something akin to panic, he realized she was going to leave. He moved fast, cutting her off at the door, taking hold of her arms. "Where are you going?"

"Home, of course."

"We've got to talk about this."

"What's there to say?" she said, her expression stoic. "I just thought you had a right to know."

"But you can't just walk in here, drop this bomb and go."

"Why not? It's not as if I'm asking for anything from you."

"Not asking?" Gray could feel the pulse pounding in his temples. "You don't have to *ask* for anything. This is my child. I'll do—"

"Don't say it!" Kathryn interrupted, jerking herself out of his grasp. "Don't you dare tell me you'll *do the right thing.*"

"But Kathryn..." Gray began, reaching for her again.

She held him off with a hand that trembled. "Just stop it. I don't want you to do your duty. I'm not interested in my child becoming another one of your many responsibilities."

"It's *our* child," he said, gently pushing her restraining arm out of the way. "And I will do what's right."

Kathryn backed all the way to the counter, holding Gray off. Tears were threatening to overflow her eyes, though she was fighting them with all her might. "I don't want you to do what's right. I want you to say you love me, that you want this child. But I know that's not going to happen."

At that moment, Gray wanted to tell her exactly what she wanted to hear. Even more, he wanted to believe in that fragile, elusive emotion she called love. He wanted to make promises about building a life together, about raising their child. But he didn't trust in promises like that. Nothing in his life had shown him that he could trust in love.

If love was real, Gray's father never would have left his mother to raise Gray on her own. If love was an emotion to trust in, all the men who came after Gray's father would have realized what a precious, perfect gift they were getting when his mother said she loved them. But they never did. They moved on, and so did she. And each time, when love proved false, there was a little more wreckage for Gray to tidy up, a few more stitches to put in his mother's heart.

The one time he had thought he was in love and had trusted someone to love him, Gray had been deserted and betrayed, as well. With all his hard-won wisdom, he should have known better than to give his heart. Just as he should have known all through this affair with Kathryn that he was getting in too deep, that she was beginning to care too much, that she would expect the same from him. But he was terrified of that. For once he laid his feelings bare, she could hurt him. She could leave him. She could walk out and turn her back on the inevitable messiness of life.

The words pounding inside him came out in a fierce rush as he took Kathryn by the shoulders. "I can't do it," he told her in a choked voice. "I can't let myself love you."

"Then let go of me."

"But I won't desert my child. I'm not that kind of man. Please, Kathryn…"

She wasn't listening to him. Kathryn realized that she had come over here for all the wrong reasons. She had told herself she just wanted Gray to know about the baby, but now she faced the reality that she wanted much more.

"I thought this would make a difference," she said through her tears. "I thought once you heard about the baby—"

"That I'd fall at your feet," he suggested bitterly.

His choice of words sent anger surging through Kathryn, drying her tears. She managed to twist from his grasp once again. "I don't want you at my feet," she snapped. "I wanted you at my side."

"And you thought a baby would ensure that?"

"What are you implying?"

His lips had compressed to a hard line. "Maybe that this baby wasn't an accident."

She slapped him. She'd raised her hand, swung it toward his chin, felt his flinch, heard the smack of skin against skin and been prepared to hit him again before Gray grabbed her arm. Then Kathryn fell back, shocked.

She began to shake, even as Gray's expression dissolved from suspicion to remorse. "God, Kathryn, I didn't mean to say that to you. I'm just not thinking straight. I don't really think you'd do this on purpose. I'm sorry. Please forgive me...I'm sorry."

Kathryn barely heard him. She had never hit anyone. Even when her ex-husband had hit her, she had never raised a hand to him. She knew she had to get out of here or something terrible was going to happen.

"Let me go," she told Gray. "Right now."

He released her with no argument, and with head held high, she stalked away.

"Don't think this is the end of this," Gray called after her. "We have to talk."

Resolutely, she continued across the kitchen and onto the utility porch, with Gray trailing.

"It's my baby, too," he shouted just before she slammed the screen door.

For a moment, Gray sagged against the door. He watched Kathryn get in her car, gun the motor and leave. Then he turned.

He found Ashley and Jarrett staring at him.

"What baby?" his sister asked.

"Kathryn's baby?" Jarrett added. "Yours and Kathryn's?"

Gray didn't bother with prevarications. He nodded.

Jarrett released a long, low whistle. There was something altogether too pleased about the look on his face. "My, my, my. And to think you accused us of being irresponsible."

Kathryn didn't remember driving home. One minute she was flying down Gray's drive, the next she was dragging herself up the stairs to her apartment. She fell on the sofa, not even bothering to turn on the lights.

She lay in the dark for a long, long time. She cried some, but mainly she was silent, listening to the air conditioner do battle with the muggy Texas night. She finally slept, too exhausted to go to her bed.

She woke up to the same set of problems. Incredibly, she thought about calling her parents. They would have to know about the baby, she supposed. There wasn't much interaction between the population of Amarillo and Fort Worth, but the word would get out some way. And surely they would want to know their grandchild.

The moment that thought was formed, Kathryn knew it was ridiculous. Her mother and father wouldn't want an illegitimate grandchild any more than they had wanted the one she had conceived with Darren. *That cretin's child* was how her mother had referred to the boy Kathryn had miscarried. Kathryn shuddered to think what her mother would call this baby. With surprise, she found herself wishing that her mother would call this baby "grandchild."

"This baby. My baby," Kathryn crooned, curving her hands over her stomach.

The baby would be hers and hers alone. She would tell Devon the news today. Then she would call Paige in California. Once they got over their shock, these two women, her best friends, would be happy for her, strong for her. Kathryn had other friends who would help, as well. She wasn't isolated and alone, the way she had been when she was married to Darren.

And perhaps it was time to reach out to her parents and brother, as well. Gray had kept his family together against big odds. Kathryn thought she had learned from that.

Her resolve concerning Gray and their child wavered. Then Kathryn remembered his accusation that she became pregnant on purpose.

She would close him out, she vowed. After what he

had said last night, he didn't deserve to be part of this child's life. Kathryn didn't need his help. And she would rather the baby didn't know his father if Gray were to act out of merely a sense of duty instead of love.

Stubbornly, Kathryn tried to close her mind to the loving side she knew Gray had. She had seen it in action with Ashley and Rick. His sense of responsibility toward his siblings was well-developed, but he loved them, too. Fiercely. Alone, he had raised Ashley from the age of eleven, Rick from the age of one, under difficult circumstances. He admitted he had made his share of mistakes, but not loving his brother and sister wasn't one of them. Gray had already proven himself a wonderful father figure. She knew he would be the same to his child.

"This child. Gray's child." Once more, Kathryn pressed her hand against her abdomen.

God help her. She couldn't shut Gray out of this child's life.

But that meant he would have to be a part of hers, as well. She would have to live, up close and personal, with loving him in vain.

Swinging her legs to the floor in front of the sofa, Kathryn sat up. She wished she didn't love Gray. She wished she could focus on all his flaws, like his stubbornness and his inability to deal with or express his feelings. But all of that was overshadowed by his kindness and his innate honesty. Damn it, why did he have to be such a decent man? So strong and direct. So complex and yet simple. What you saw was what you got. And she loved him.

With elbows braced on her thighs, Kathryn leaned forward and put her face in her hands. She stayed that way until someone banged on her door. Until Gray called her name.

"Open up," he demanded when she hesitated. In a low but clear tone, he added, "Open this damn door or I'll knock it down."

She shoved a hand through her tousled hair, pulled in a deep breath and opened the door, prepared to face another round of Gray's anger.

What she found instead were flowers. A huge sheaf of them, held out to her by Gray. His expression was serious, not angry. His voice was steady when he said, "You have to forgive me, Kathryn. I didn't mean what I said to you about planning this. I know you wouldn't do that."

Not answering, she took the flowers and stepped aside for him to enter the apartment while she closed the door.

He stood in the center of the room, looking awkward and somewhat fearful.

Kathryn didn't know what to say. All she knew was she didn't want to argue anymore.

Gray got right to the point. "Marry me," he said.

And for a moment, hope bloomed inside Kathryn, as bright and fresh as the blossoms she held.

Chapter Ten

"You have to marry me."

Gray's command sent Kathryn's foolish hopes tumbling again. Despite the flowers, despite his absence of anger, nothing had changed since last night. Far from declaring a newly discovered love for her, Gray was just playing lord and master, a part he had down pat.

"I thought about this all night. Marriage is our only option."

She very carefully placed the flowers on a table near the door and smoothed a hand down her rumpled clothes. She wished she'd had a chance to freshen up before Gray came barging in like this. She badly needed to get herself together.

"Aren't you going to say something?" Gray demanded.

Kathryn didn't look up. "No."

"But we have to talk—"

"There's nothing to say," she interrupted, turning toward him again. "I'm not going to marry you. And that's final."

He lifted his hands in a futile gesture. "You're not thinking this through. For the baby's sake, we need to look at this logically."

"Thinking this through is all I've been doing since I left your place last night."

Concern knit his brow. "You don't look as if you've slept a wink. You've got to take better care of yourself, Kathryn."

She started a protest that he dismissed quickly.

"You need rest. I bet you slept right here on the sofa, and that's not good—"

She brushed his instructions aside. "Don't be giving me orders on how to take care of myself, Gray Nolan. As I've said before, you're not my boss."

"You're pregnant. You need someone to look after you."

"Don't be such a big, macho jerk," she retorted. "Being pregnant doesn't turn a woman into an invalid."

Now he looked irritated. "I'm just concerned. Despite what you think, I care about you. I don't want anything to happen to you, or to our child, and I don't believe I'm out of line in worrying about you."

"Do you think I'd endanger myself or this baby?" she demanded, her fury mounting.

"Not intentionally, but you're emotional and overwrought—"

"I am not," she shouted, her tone negating her words.

"Just listen to yourself," he shot back. "You need to calm down."

"And you need to take your flowers and your matrimonial orders and get out of here." Her head was buzzing with anger as she stalked to the door. "I don't have time to listen to anyone who thinks I'd take any chances on losing another baby." She flung open the door.

But Gray didn't move. He was as still as the hot summer morning simmering outside. "*Another* baby?" he said, staring at her.

Only then did Kathryn realize what she had said.

"You lost a baby?" Gray repeated when she didn't speak.

Kathryn took a long, calming breath. Very slowly, she closed the door again and faced Gray. She knew him well enough to know he wouldn't leave before she gave him an explanation. "I lost a baby with my first husband."

"You never said anything about that before."

She shrugged. "It wasn't…" The words stuck in her throat.

"Don't say it wasn't important," Gray said, moving toward her again. "Of course it was. I can see by your face that it almost killed you."

He read her too well, as usual, even when she was trying so desperately to hide her emotions. She moved away from him, coming to rest behind a chair as if that could protect her from his intense, probing regard. "Just go," she told him. "I don't want to talk about this."

But he wasn't leaving. "What happened?" he asked. "Is it something we should worry about this time?"

She managed a short, mirthless laugh. "Not unless you're planning to throw me up against a wall a half-dozen times."

"What?" The word, like Gray's features, was infused with horror.

Kathryn had never intended to tell Gray about her miscarriage. She had told him that Darren was abusive, but what her ex-husband had done to her and her child was in the past and was best left there.

Of course Gray wasn't content to know only the bare facts. He came around the chair, eyes blazing, though his touch to her shoulders was infinitely tender. "What did that bastard do to you?"

"Just what I said," she replied as calmly as possible. "He went into a rage and banged me up against the wall of our apartment. He hit me hard enough to cause a miscarriage."

"God." Groaning, Gray wrapped his arms around her, drawing her close.

Kathryn wanted to resist, but couldn't. She accepted his comfort, even reveled in it. Few people knew the depth of agony she had suffered at Darren's hands. Those that did—her parents, especially—had been unable to comfort her. There was a part of her that wanted to stay in Gray's arms forever.

Gray was still ranting against Darren when her thoughts returned to the present. "How could he do that? How could a man destroy his own child? No matter what kind of man he was, if he knew you were pregnant—"

"But that was why," Kathryn murmured against his chest.

Easing her away, Gray stared down at her. "What?"

"He didn't want a child. Neither did I, at first. I mean, we were kids. My parents had practically disowned me. We didn't have much money..." She paused to take a deep breath. "But of course, after I was pregnant, I wanted the child. I hid the pregnancy from Darren for almost four months. But when I had to tell him, he was so mad..." She flinched, recalling in vivid detail Darren's fury. "He said I got pregnant on purpose."

If Gray had been horrified before, he now crossed over into a new dimension. He retreated from Kathryn, his face a study in guilt and pain. "I said the same thing to you last night."

Kathryn nodded.

"I didn't mean it."

"I know that," she assured him. "And even if you did, you would never—"

"I would never, ever hurt you," Gray completed. "Please say you know that."

She summoned a tremulous smile. "Of course you couldn't. That never entered my mind."

"But I said those words," Gray muttered grimly. "I said the same thing to you as he did. No wonder you hit me."

Kathryn clasped her hands together. "I shouldn't have done that. I've never hit anyone before."

"I deserved worse."

"That's not true. Nobody deserves violence of any kind."

"Except maybe your ex-husband."

She whirled away. "Let's forget him, please. Let's not mention Darren again. I put him and what happened behind me a long, long time ago. I divorced him. I finished school. I moved here and I've gone on with my life. He is history. If I keep dredging him up, that means he still owns a piece of my soul."

Gray agreed not to mention her ex-husband again. But as he stood looking at Kathryn's slender back, he couldn't help wishing he could get his hands on the man who had hurt her. He also couldn't stop berating himself for his foolhardy accusation about her planning this pregnancy. He'd had every opportunity to stop before they made love without protection. This mess was as much his fault as hers.

Perhaps if he had never suspected his own mother of using a pregnancy to trap a man, he wouldn't have been in such a rush to judgment with Kathryn. But Kathryn wouldn't do that. She wasn't like his mother. Gray realized he needed to let go of the past once and for all. The important thing now was to do the right thing about the future. That brought Gray back to his purpose in being here this morning.

"I know you don't want to hear this," he said quietly to Kathryn, "but I want to marry you."

She turned, her face weary. "You want to give your child your name. Like always, you're trying to take care of everyone. That's noble, Gray, and so like you. But it's not what I want."

"Think of the baby and what's right for him. I know what it's like to be without a father. I can't do that to my child." His resolve hardened into steel. "I won't do it."

"The baby won't be without a father. Last night, I wanted to cut you out of our lives, but I know that's not right. You'll be a part of his life, Gray. A big part."

"So you're suggesting we do a nineties kind of thing? You live with the baby alone. I visit every other weekend." Gray found the idea distasteful. He wanted his child under his roof, all the time. "No thank you."

"It wouldn't be impossible."

"But why do that when we could get married?" His voice lowered, deepened. "I know you want all the

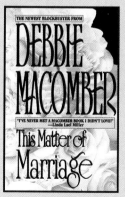

This Matter of Marriage

**delivers warmth, humor, romance—
a definite "feel-good" reading experience!**

From Hallie McCarthy's Diary:

A new year generally starts out with me writing a few inspiring lines about how I'm going to lose five pounds—let's be honest, it's ten—and pay off all my credit cards, and other high expections like that. It's the same every January. But *this* year's going to be different.

Oh, I still want to lose those extra pounds, more than ever, but for a different reason.

I want a husband. And eventually a family.

And that means I need a plan. Being a goal-oriented person, I start by identifying what I'm after (MARRIAGE!) and then I work out a logical procedure for getting it. Which, in this case, includes *looking good*. (Not that I look bad now, if I do say so myself. But I'm talking *really* good. Are you listening, thighs?) Because, as I've learned in advertising, *packaging counts*.

So, last week I made *the* decision: *Marriage!*

And be sure to look for Debbie's October 1997 title, THREE BRIDES, NO GROOM...three brand-new stories of three friends who discover that Mr. Right has turned into Mr. Wrong...but that doesn't stop them from finding true love—and marriage.

romantic hearts and flowers, Kathryn. All the stuff I can't promise. But I could give you and the baby a home. We could be a real family. I've never been part of a conventional family, but I'm willing to try."

"No deal, Gray. Not unless I can have your heart as part of the package."

Her stubbornness brought his temper to the simmering point again. By sheer force of will, he held the lid on and tried a new tack. He put out his hand, taking hers. "We have a lot going for us."

"Not enough, obviously."

He drew her into the circle of his arms and lowered his mouth toward hers. "We have this."

Kathryn pulled away before the kiss could deepen in the way of most of their kisses. "Passion isn't enough, Gray."

"It's more than some people have."

"It's not all I want," she insisted.

"But it's what I can give," Gray cried, frustration escaping his tightly corked emotions. "I can give you passion. I can give you my name, my fidelity, my care. Those are things that matter."

"But all of that, without your love, without that ultimate trust, is empty." Kathryn's eyes were deep green pools of sadness. "I grew up in an empty home, Gray. My parents don't love each other. The only reason they're still married is because keeping up appearances is so important to them. Maybe there was a time, when my brother and I were younger perhaps, that Mother and Father were close, maybe even loving. But that was gone long ago. What's left behind is very cold. I don't want to end up that way. I don't want our child to see us end up that way, either."

"So it's better if he sees us living apart, never married?"

"At least then we won't be living a lie."

"I think we're cheating him."

Kathryn agreed. "That's something I suppose we should have thought about before we started playing Russian roulette with your sperm."

"I'd give anything to take back what's happened," Gray murmured.

"Would you?" Sadness easing from her beautiful eyes, Kathryn lifted a hand to his cheek. "Even now, with all of this to face, I wouldn't trade that afternoon with you."

Looking down at her, it was easy for Gray to remember that day, the swirling vortex of desire that had pulled them both into foolhardy danger. Perhaps the present consequences were a small price for having known that kind of passion.

"I wouldn't trade this child, either," Kathryn said.

He covered her hand with his, turning his head so that his lips pressed against her open palm. A torrent of confusing emotions swirled inside him. It would be easy, all too easy, to make the promises she needed from him. If he believed in love the way she did, he could let go of the iron bands around his heart. But his doubts and fears gripped him as tightly as ever. His hard-won life experiences told him not to trust the tenderness that threatened to overtake him. How could he let go of the truths he had believed for so very long?

Kathryn must have sensed the battle waging inside him. For she said, "You can't force it, Gray. If it's not meant to be, then that's all there is to it. Love either is, or it isn't. It's that simple and that difficult."

The nervous energy that had carried him through a

sleepless night and brought him to her door deserted Gray in a hurry. He felt his shoulders slump with a weariness that overtook every muscle in his body. "There's nothing I can say, is there?" he asked Kathryn.

She said no.

He tried to form another protest but couldn't. He found the way they stood here, so close and yet so completely apart, to be infinitely sad. When the silence had stretched to the breaking point, he said, "Where do we go from here?"

"I need some time. Some space to sort everything out."

His denial was quick. "You can't be alone."

She was beginning a protest when a knock sounded at the door. Looking almost relieved, Kathryn rushed to open it.

Rick ran straight into her arms, calling her name like a prayer.

Behind the boy stood an apologetic Mary Green. "I'm sorry to be on your doorstep before nine in the morning," she said, looking from Gray to Kathryn. "But Rick insisted that I bring him here instead of taking him to camp or home."

"I wanted to see Kathryn," the boy said, raising his head from where he had burrowed it in Kathryn's side. He glowered at Gray. "You said I couldn't see her."

To Gray, Mary continued her apology. "You know I wouldn't have done this normally, no matter how much he begged. But when I saw your Jeep parked here, I decided to give in." A glint of disapproval entered her kind blue eyes. "Gray, you and Kathryn need to sit down and talk to Rick. He needs to know what's going on with you. He deserves your honesty."

"I should have come to see you," Kathryn said to Rick as she stroked his hair. "I'm sorry."

"I missed you," he said, his voice catching on a sob.

Gray, fearing a scene was about to begin, turned to Mary. "You're right about this. Thanks for bringing him by."

The woman reached out and gripped his hand. "I hope this works out." She sent a brief, encouraging smile toward Kathryn, leaving Gray to wonder exactly what Mary was hoping for.

Once she was gone, Gray turned back to Rick. "Come on," he said, holding out his hand. "Let's sit over here on the sofa and talk."

Rick pressed himself tighter to Kathryn's side. "I don't want to talk to you."

"Then talk to me," Kathryn said with just the right mix of authority and gentleness.

Funny how she had known just how to talk to the boy. Right from the start, Gray marveled.

Kathryn led Rick to the sofa, sat him down, then perched on the edge of the coffee table facing him. "Now, what's wrong?"

"Gray said we weren't going to see you anymore." Again the boy shot a baleful glance at his big brother.

"You can see me," Kathryn replied. "If your brother says it's okay."

Gray nodded. *Why try to keep them apart when his and Kathryn's baby would be part of Rick's family.*

She continued talking to Rick. "I want to see you, too. But things are going to be different than they were."

"How?"

"Well...for one thing, when I see you, it'll probably just be me and you."

"Gray won't be there?"

"Not most of the time."

"Why?"

"Because Gray and I aren't..." Kathryn hesitated as if fumbling for the right word. "Gray and I are just not going to see each other anymore."

"Why?"

Gray stepped in. "What Kathryn means is that she and I won't be going on dates." *But we are going to have a baby together.* Explaining that was going to be a real trick. And if Rick couldn't comprehend what in the hell they were doing, then how was their child ever going to understand?

Rick's blue eyes narrowed as he gazed at his brother. "So you're not going to marry her?"

"No."

The boy turned back to Kathryn. His lower lip trembled. "Don't you love us?"

She chucked him under the chin. "Of course. I love you very much."

The boy mulled that over for a few moments, then offered, "We have room for you at our house. You can hang clothes in my closet." His gaze fastened on the glass globe, which had fascinated him ever since his first visit to her apartment. "And there's room for all of your stuff. Gray will let you sleep with him like always."

Gray looked at Kathryn. *And we thought we were hiding so much from him,* he communicated with his eyes.

Her face flushed, Kathryn assured Rick, "I know you have room. That's not the problem."

"I don't understand," Rick said, looking first at Kathryn and then at Gray. "Mary says when people love each other, they usually get married."

"We're not getting married," Gray said with quiet command.

"But I want you to." Rick's eyes filled with tears as he looked accusingly at Gray. "I told all my friends that Kathryn was going to be my big sister, older than Ashley, almost like a mom. That's what I want."

"You and I will still be friends," Kathryn told him soothingly. "Just like Gray and I will be friends."

"It's not the same," Rick said. Pulling free of Kathryn's grasp, he scooted off the sofa and faced the two adults with hands clenched at his sides. "It's not right."

"Just calm down." Gray reached out to take the boy's arm, but he wrenched away.

"I don't believe you love me," Rick shouted at Kathryn. "I'm the reason you don't want to marry Gray."

She stood, moving toward him quickly. "That's not true."

"I'm just a bunch of trouble," Rick yelled at her. "I'm the reason Gray didn't marry Gina, and now you don't want us, either. And it's all my fault, I know."

"Gina?" Gray questioned, brought to a halt by the mention of his ex-fiancée.

Tears streaming down his face, Rick faced his brother again. "I heard you and Ashley talking. You said Gina didn't want me, and that's why she left."

"No," Gray said, finally taking hold of the boy. "It was me she didn't want. Just me. It had nothing to do with you. Listen to me, Rick. That had nothing to do with you. Me and Kathryn not getting married has nothing to do with you, either. Didn't you hear her? She loves you, Rick.''

"I don't believe you," Rick screamed. "Or Kathryn, either. You're both dirty liars. I hate you both." Kicking and punching, he managed to break free of Gray once again.

But Kathryn caught him. Saying his name over and over, she tried in vain to get him to look at her, to listen to her calming words of love and reassurance.

Rick, however, was in that place of loss and pain where he sometimes went. A place where no one seemed able to reach him. He struggled and stumbled out of Kathryn's arms, then backward, falling against the pedestal where the glass globe sat.

For a long, breathless moment, the globe danced on top of its marble platform. Gray leaped forward, trying to reach it.

But he was too late.

The globe bounced against the wall, then onto the base of the pedestal. The delicate glass shattered into hundreds of tiny pieces around Rick, who sprawled on the floor.

Kathryn gasped.

Gray swore.

Rick froze, staring first at the glass that surrounded him, then at Kathryn. His eyes, tearless now, grew round and wide. "I'm sorry," he mumbled.

Kathryn nodded. Gray saw the muscles working in her throat.

Maybe if she could have said something, Rick might not have run. But her silence seemed to propel him forward. He scrambled to his feet in the mess of broken glass and shot past Gray's grabbing arm and to the door, flinging it open.

"Go get him," Kathryn ordered Gray. "Get him now."

Not having waited for her urging, Gray was already at the door. He thundered down the steep outdoor steps, calling for his brother, who sped nimbly ahead. Gray reached the bottom just a step behind Rick. At the edge of the back, private driveway, he was able to reach out and get hold of Rick's shirt, then his arm. Gray pulled the boy up and into his arms. He held him there tightly, stroking his back, telling him it would be all right until the fight went out of Rick's sturdy little body and he began to sob.

From the top of the stairs, Kathryn called, "Rick, are you all right?" She clattered down the stairs. "Did any of that glass cut you?"

Gray turned to find her halfway down the steps. He opened his mouth to tell her to be careful.

But Kathryn was already falling. Like a child's toy, she bounced down the steps, landing on her back at the bottom.

And somewhere, between the edge of the driveway where he dropped Rick to his feet and the spot where Kathryn lay, the iron bars around Gray's heart came undone. He knew, with a terrible certainty, what he had tried to deny for these past months.

He loved her.

He loved her with all the fury, all the aching need, all the elusive power and sweet intensity that he had said were figments of other people's fancy.

Dropping to his knees at her side, he kept saying the words over and over. "I love you, Kathryn. Please be okay so I can tell you how much I love you."

Just as he touched her, she stirred, looking up at him with glazed eyes. But something akin to a smile twitched her lips. "I'm not unconscious," she muttered. "I heard what you said. You can't deny it later."

"Just be still," Gray said, moving his hands over her body in search of broken bones.

"I'm okay," she said, wincing as his fingers skimmed over an abrasion on her knee. "Just keep saying you love me."

Their eyes met and held as Gray obeyed her command.

Rick ran up sobbing and dropped to the ground beside her. "Are you okay? Please be okay, Kathryn. I'm so sorry."

Kathryn reached out and, over Gray's protests, drew Rick to her, pressing his hot, wet face to her neck. "I'm fine," she said. "I'm just fine."

Then she looked at Gray. Her face had gone pale, with lines bracketing each side of her mouth. "Let Rick sit with me. You go call an ambulance. Tell them...tell them to take care of my baby." Then she closed her eyes and held on to Rick. As if for dear life.

Gray shot up the stairs like a man from a circus cannon.

She wasn't losing this baby.

Not his baby.

Not now that he knew he loved her so much.

Chapter Eleven

Awakening in the gloomy twilight of her bedroom, Kathryn stretched before she remembered her injuries. Her muscles protested, and she groaned just as she caught sight of the somber little boy who hovered in the doorway.

"I'm really, really sorry about the globe," he said.

"I know." Kathryn pushed herself up on her pillows and gestured for him to join her. "Come here."

Rick went into her arms without hesitation. He trembled a bit, no doubt trying to hold back his tears. Despite her aches and pains, Kathryn gave him a long, hard hug. Then he sat back and regarded her with a gloomy expression.

"Hey, now," she murmured, "you need to be smiling. You didn't cut yourself to ribbons on that broken glass, and all I did was bruise some ribs."

From the side of the bed where she snapped on the

bedside lamp, Ashley spoke up. "He's been worrying all afternoon about how Gray's going to punish him."

Kathryn tweaked Rick lightly on the nose. "I'm going to see if I can't get you off easy. I think the day you've been through should be punishment enough."

But Rick shook his head. "I deserve to be punished for breaking the globe your grandmother gave you."

"Well…" Kathryn sighed, looking the boy straight in the eye. "I'm not going to pretend I won't miss it."

His expression fiercely determined, Rick said, "Someday I'm going to France and get you a new one."

"Sounds like a good deal to me."

Jarrett appeared in the doorway, his broad shoulders practically filling the narrow space. "You doing okay, Kathryn?"

"Just groggy and aching a little."

"I had a busted rib once," the young man said as he ambled into the room. "I was trying to break a horse and got thrown right on top of the fence."

Rick's eyes grew round. "Really? Cool."

Ashley tsk-tsked. "No, it's not cool, Rick. So don't be jumping on any strange horses any time soon."

"Come on," Jarrett invited, gesturing for Rick to follow him. "Let's go outside and I'll show you how it happened."

Kathryn flinched as Rick's enthusiastic jump off the bed jostled her aching rib cage. "Wait a minute," she called after him. He paused in the door. "Come back here." Rick obeyed, and she reached out to squeeze his hand. In her most serious voice, she said, "I hope today set you straight about a few things…like how much I love you."

He nodded, hugged her again and then was off to

hear about more important matters, like bustin' broncos. But Kathryn knew he had heard her, and more importantly, she felt he really believed her.

Ashley sat down in the chair beside her bed. "Are you really okay?"

"Absolutely."

"And the baby?"

Shocked, Kathryn stared at her.

Ashley quickly explained how she and Jarrett had heard them arguing the night before. "Jarrett and I were really surprised," Ashley said. "After the way Gray ragged on us all summer, telling us to be careful, then you get pregnant."

"Are you upset about it?" Kathryn asked.

"Of course not," Ashley replied. "As long as you and Gray work all this out between you, I don't care how many babies you have."

Pleased, Kathryn eased back on her pillows again. "Where is Gray?" She peered around Ashley toward the dimly lit apartment beyond her bedroom door. "I vaguely remember him bringing me home from the hospital. Then I think I passed out." *She needed to see Gray. They had a lot to sort out.*

Getting up to rearrange the flowers someone had placed in a vase beside the bed, Ashley smiled. "I have this feeling my big brother's gone somewhere to fall apart for a while. You know he doesn't do that in front of other people. He was really relieved when you turned out to be okay."

With a tender, secret smile, Kathryn wondered what Ashley would think if she knew how Gray had cried earlier today when her injuries proved minor and the doctor pronounced the baby unharmed. Both of them had fallen apart from relief. She thought, however, that was one side of Gray that she should keep from his sister.

"Gray should be back sometime soon," Ashley continued. "He asked me and Rick to stay here with you. Devon took care of the shop all day. Jarrett came by to..." Pausing for a moment, Ashley flipped a long tendril of blond hair over her shoulder. She took a deep breath. "Jarrett came by to cancel the tuxedo rentals for the wedding."

"Cancel, huh?" Kathryn sighed. "So it's really off?"

"For now."

"But you and Jarrett seem okay about it. He was here. You're talking to each other."

"Your getting pregnant convinced us to wait."

"How's that?"

Edging carefully onto the side of the bed, Ashley explained. "Last night, after Gray made me and Jarrett talk, we thought we might go ahead. Then we heard you and Gray arguing. We found out you were having a baby. We saw how torn up you both were, and then...we just knew." Ashley paused, her mouth trembling slightly.

Kathryn reached out and took her hand. "What did you know?"

Ashley wiped away a tear that escaped from the corner of one eye. "We've always been so careful...you know. But even so, knowing you and Gray made a mistake...well, it made us think we could, too. And even if we were married, that could mess up a lot of stuff. School. And traveling. And all the stuff we want to do."

"So you're going to wait?"

Nodding, Ashley squeezed her eyes shut against

fresh tears. "We're not ready, Kathryn. Not by a long shot."

"You might be someday."

"But I may lose him."

"And you love him a lot?"

"I think more than he loves me. I talked to his dad today. He says Jarrett's restless and I should just give him some space."

"Men can be slow. Give him time to go along with that space."

Quickly brushing tears off her cheeks, Ashley got hold of herself. "Will you keep my dress for me?"

"Of course."

The younger woman's beautiful smile lit up the room. "I'm still going to have my dream wedding...someday."

"And whoever is waiting at the altar will be a lucky guy."

The two of them were laughing softly when Gray appeared in the doorway. "This looks like girl talk," he said. "Should I leave and come back?"

"No way," Kathryn said, not bothering to disguise her pleasure at the sight of him.

Ashley went over to give him a swift hug and firm instructions. "You be nice to her."

"I promise," Gray said, surprised by his sister's display of affection.

"I'm taking charge of Rick for the entire night," Ashley added with a tart look at Gray and Kathryn. "I expect the two of you to put this time to wise use."

Then she left, calling for her younger brother, slamming the door on the way out.

Gray breathed a sigh of relief. "That's good. Without the slam, I would have known for sure an alien being had taken over my sister's body.''

"I told you she'd be human again one day.''

"She's human, and the wedding's off.''

"So you're a happy man.''

"I will be when I can hold you.''

In answer, Kathryn held out her arms.

"But you're hurt.''

"I'll hurt more if you don't kiss me pretty soon.''

He obeyed, sitting gingerly on the bed and gently enfolding her in his embrace. Strangely enough, however, all thoughts of treating Kathryn with kid gloves soon fled Gray's mind. He didn't stop kissing her until she groaned.

"I'm sorry," he muttered, drawing back.

But she locked her arms around his neck. "That was a groan of pleasure, not pain.''

With infinite care, Gray traced a finger from her collarbone, down the fragile silk of her gown, around one sweetly-peaking nipple, and came to rest on the tight wrap bound around her ribs. Softly, he said, "I thought I would die when you fell down those steps.''

"I'm glad you didn't.''

"I'm sorry about all of this. Rick pitching a fit, breaking that gift from your grandmother—''

"Shh." Kathryn placed two fingers against his lips. "There are no apologies needed for that. He was very upset. He didn't mean to do it. Rick would never destroy something I loved on purpose. For all his troubles, he doesn't have that in him.''

Gray took her hand, threading his fingers through hers. "Rick and I are quite a pair, you know. Sometimes we don't know whom or what to trust.''

"People have let you down in the past.''

"But I think...I know now...that we can both count on you."

"Forever," she said.

"So, this is the thing." Gray reached into his pocket and took out a ring. "I want you to wear this, Kathryn. I want you to marry me." The ring was a diamond, the biggest he had been able to afford at the closest jewelry store he had been able to find open this afternoon when Kathryn went to sleep.

Kathryn was staring at the ring as if it was alive.

"If you don't like it..." Gray began.

"Of course I like it," she said. "No woman in her right mind wouldn't like that ring."

"Then you'll wear it? You'll marry me?"

She hesitated, and Gray felt his heart rate plunge. *What was the matter?*

"First, I have to know something," Kathryn murmured, her gaze fixed on his. "What made you sure you loved me?"

"I don't know exactly."

"But you have to have a clue. Was it because you were so afraid I was hurt, that the baby was hurt?"

He shook his head, chuckling suddenly. "It was the mess, I think."

She frowned. "What mess?"

"The whole damned mess. You being pregnant. Rick flipping out. You falling down the stairs. I think I decided the whole damned jumble just fitted too perfectly into my crazy mess of a life. I finally knew that you fitted, too. So I decided this must be love."

"That's very strange," Kathryn said, not looking very pleased.

"So you don't want this ring?" he asked, starting to put it back in his pocket.

She stuck out her hand again. "I didn't say that."

He put it on her finger, laid her back against her pillows and kissed her. Every inch of her. From her mouth to her bruised ribs to her scraped knees to the still-flat belly under which his baby was still growing, safe and sound. Slowly and carefully and with great patience, Gray let his mouth explore regions heretofore unknown.

To Kathryn's great delight, that took most of the night.

Three weeks later, on the last Saturday in August, in the chapel the groom's sister had reserved for her now-canceled dream wedding, Dr. Gray Nolan married Miss Kathryn Seeger.

Miss Seeger was attended by her best friend, Paige McMullen, of Santa Monica, California. Like the grown-up tomboy she was, Paige forgot her shoes and had to borrow a pair from a guest before her walk down the aisle. Later, barefoot, she danced with everyone who asked, although her gaze was most often on an old friend, a big, husky rancher named True Whitman, who *didn't* ask.

Devon Long, the bride's business associate, directed the wedding and reception as well as serving as brides-maid. But instead of overseeing the food, she spent an inordinate amount of time with a tall, dark-haired stranger who neither the bride nor the groom knew. A stranger who disappeared, along with Devon, long before the reception was over.

Ashley Grant, bridesmaid and newly unengaged college freshman, wore a sophisticated fuchsia gown that earned her plenty of looks from the crowd of West Texas studs in attendance. That made her ex-fiancé,

Jarrett McMullen, madder than hell. He went storming off, but everyone agreed that his and Ashley's story wasn't over. Not quite.

As for the bride and groom and the rest of the wedding…

She was afflicted with afternoon sickness.

He was late, having spent the morning performing emergency surgery on a prize bull.

The air conditioner in the church shut off, forcing the temperature up near one hundred degrees, which was about normal for August in Amarillo.

And the heat melted the chocolate icing on the groom's cake.

Which was just as well, since the groom's young brother and two of his friends were practicing their third-base slides in the reception hall and sent that cake flying.

Asked later to assess the various disasters that attended the wedding she had dreamed of all her life, the bride just looked deeply into her adoring groom's eyes and said, "Well, that's life, you know. Pretty messy. But awfully precious."

It was about that time that the groom swept her up in his arms and carried her out of the reception, forgoing the traditional throwing of the bouquet and the dousing of the happy couple with rice. Everyone there heard him say he was taking her straight to bed.

Some folks were scandalized. Most just grinned.

For they knew where the best of dream weddings should end.

*   *   *   *   *

Silhouette's newest series

YOURS TRULY

Love when you least expect it.

Where the written word plays a vital role in uniting couples—you're guaranteed a fun and exciting read every time!

Look for Marie Ferrarella's upcoming Yours Truly, *Traci on the Spot*, in March 1997.

Here's a special sneak preview....

1

Morgan Brigham slowly set down his coffee cup on the kitchen table and stared at the comic strip in the center of his paper. It was nestled in among approximately twenty others that were spread out across two pages. But this was the only one he made a point of reading faithfully each morning at breakfast.

This was the only one that mirrored *her* life.

He read each panel twice, as if he couldn't trust his own eyes. But he could. It was there, in black and white.

Morgan folded the paper slowly, thoughtfully, his mind not on his task. So Traci was getting engaged.

The realization gnawed at the lining of his stomach. He hadn't a clue as to why.

He had even less of a clue why he did what he did next.

Abandoning his coffee, now cool, and the newspaper, and ignoring the fact that this was going to make him late for the office, Morgan went to get a sheet of stationery from the den.

He didn't have much time.

Traci Richardson stared at the last frame she had just drawn. Debating, she glanced at the creature sprawled out on the kitchen floor.

"What do you think, Jeremiah? Too blunt?"

The dog, part bloodhound, part mutt, idly looked up from his rawhide bone at the sound of his name. Jeremiah gave her a look she felt free to interpret as ambivalent.

"Fine help you are. What if Daniel actually reads this and puts two and two together?"

Not that there was all that much chance that the man who had proposed to her, the very prosperous and busy Dr. Daniel Thane, would actually see the comic strip she drew for a living. Not unless the strip was taped to a bicuspid he was examining. Lately Daniel had gotten so busy he'd stopped reading anything but the morning headlines of the *Times*.

Still, you never knew. "I don't want to hurt his feelings," Traci continued, using Jeremiah as a sounding board. "It's just that Traci is overwhelmed by Donald's proposal and, see, she thinks the ring is going to swallow her up." To prove her point, Traci held up the drawing for the dog to view.

This time, he didn't even bother to lift his head.

Traci stared moodily at the small velvet box on the kitchen counter. It had sat there since Daniel had asked her to marry him last Sunday. Even if Daniel never read her comic strip, he was going to suspect something eventually. The very fact that she hadn't grabbed the ring from his hand and slid it onto her finger should have told him that she had doubts about their union.

Traci sighed. Daniel was a catch by any definition. So what was her problem? She kept waiting to be struck by that sunny ray of happiness. Daniel said he wanted to take care of her, to fulfill her every wish.

And he was even willing to let her think about it before she gave him her answer.

Guilt nibbled at her. She should be dancing up and down, not wavering like a weather vane in a gale.

Pronouncing the strip completed, she scribbled her signature in the corner of the last frame and then sighed. Another week's work put to bed. She glanced at the pile of mail on the counter. She'd been bringing it in steadily from the mailbox since Monday, but the stack had gotten no farther than her kitchen. Sorting letters seemed the least heinous of all the annoying chores that faced her.

Traci paused as she noted a long envelope. Morgan Brigham. Why would Morgan be writing to her?

Curious, she tore open the envelope and quickly scanned the short note inside.

Dear Traci,
I'm putting the summerhouse up for sale. Thought you might want to come up and see it one more time before it goes up on the block. Or make a bid for it yourself. If memory serves, you once said you wanted to buy it. Either way, let me know. My number's on the card.

Take care,
Morgan

P.S. Got a kick out of *Traci on the Spot* this week.

Traci folded the letter. He read her strip. She hadn't known that. A feeling of pride silently coaxed a smile to her lips. After a beat, though, the rest of his note seeped into her consciousness. He was selling the house.

The summerhouse. A faded white building with brick trim. Suddenly, memories flooded her mind. Long, lazy afternoons that felt as if they would never end.

Morgan.

She looked at the far wall in the family room. There was a large framed photograph of her and Morgan standing before the summerhouse. Traci and Morgan. Morgan and Traci. Back then, it seemed their lives had been permanently intertwined. A bittersweet feeling of loss passed over her.

Traci quickly pulled the telephone over to her on the counter and tapped out the number on the keypad.

*   *   *   *   *

Look for TRACI ON THE SPOT
by Marie Ferrarella, coming to
Silhouette YOURS TRULY
in March 1997.

Take 4 bestselling love stories FREE

Plus get a FREE surprise gift!

As seen on TV!
Free Gift Offer

With a Free Gift proof-of-purchase from any Silhouette® book,
you can receive a beautiful cubic zirconia pendant.

This gorgeous marquise-shaped stone is a genuine cubic
zirconia—accented by an 18" gold tone necklace.

(Approximate retail value $19.95)

Send for yours today...
compliments of ▼ *Silhouette*®
TM

Free Gift Certificate

Name: _____

Address: _____

City: _____ State/Province: _____ Zip/Postal Code: _____

084-KFD

By the bestselling author of *FORBIDDEN FRUIT*

FORTUNE
ERICA SPINDLER

Be careful what you wish for...

Skye Dearborn knew exactly what to wish for. To
unlock the secrets of her past. To be reunited with her
mother. To force the man who betrayed her to pay.
To be loved.

One man could make it all happen. But will Skye's
new life prove to be all that she dreamed of...or a
nightmare she can't escape?

Be careful what you wish for...it may just come true.

Available in March 1997 at your favorite retail outlet.

 MIRA The brightest star in women's fiction

Look us up on-line at: http://www.romance.net

MESF

At last the wait is over...
In March
New York Times bestselling author

NORA ROBERTS

will bring us the latest from the Stanislaskis as
Natasha's now very grown-up stepdaughter,
Freddie, and Rachel's very sexy brother-in-law
Nick discover that love is worth waiting for in

WAITING FOR NICK
Silhouette Special Edition #1088

and in April
visit Natasha and Rachel again—or meet them
for the first time—in

The Stanislaski Sisters

containing TAMING NATASHA
and FALLING FOR RACHEL

Available wherever Silhouette books are sold.